Braids In The Boardroom

Braids In The Boardroom

Thando'sJourney from Love to Leadership and Loss

Ntokozo Ncongwane

None Press

Contents

BRAIDS IN THE BOARDROOM

Thando's Journey from Love, Leadership, and Loss

Ntokozo Ncongwane

Braids in the Boardroom

Copyright @ 2024 Ntokozo Ncongwane.

ISBN -979-8-9907171-1-4

TABLE OF CONTENTS

BRAIDS IN THE BOARDROOM

Dedicated to:

The little black girl who adorns her crown in every room,
proudly and without fear,
Your rightful place is at the table, shaping the decisions for a
brighter, bolder tomorrow.

Thank You

A heartfelt appreciation goes out to our mentors and heroes, who courageously journeyed to the other side and returned to guide and support us.
Thank you, Mom. Thank you, Mr. Perkins.

HEY BLACK CHILD
by
Useni Eugene Perkins
Hey Black Child,
Do you know who you are?
Who you really are?
Do you know you can be
What you want to be?
If you try to be
what you can be.

INTRODUCTION

In the bustling classroom of Jiyana Secondary School, Thando was brimming with excitement as her English teacher, Miss Dube, shared the captivating poem of Useni Eugene Perkins with the class. Known for her unique chin beard that earned her the playful nickname 'Ntshebenyana,' Miss Dube commanded respect with her no-nonsense attitude. Initially wary of her strict demeanor, Thando and her friends were soon captivated by Miss Dube's passion for English. It transported them into a world of wonder and creativity.

Growing up in Tembisa, a small township near Johannesburg, exposed Thando to a vibrant and dynamic community. Every street corner told its story through street vendors and carefree children playing in the streets. What was true for the township was the economic challenges and social inequality that brought a sobering contrast against the otherwise thriving community.

Thando opened the last blank page in her exercise book, carefully writing her full name in cursive with pride: Thandolwethu Dhladhla, though everyone called her Thando. Only her mother and grandmother used her full name to remind her of its meaning, "Beloved to us." Teachers described Thando as a vibrant ten-year-old student who listened attentively, absorbing knowledge like a sponge.

At home, while her family engaged in animated discussions, she would curl up in a cozy nook with a book in hand, immersing herself in the pages, her eyes dancing with delight at the worlds within. Her presence was so unassuming that the family would forget she was there. Her mother was always lurking around the house. Whether vacuuming or stirring a pot, her activities filled their home with familiar sounds and comforting scents. She did not dare ask about her father's whereabouts. His sporadic absences and return with the smell of alcohol was an uncomfortable, unspoken topic. Like other uncomfortable family topics, they left that subject untouched, locked away behind the walls of their home.

Thando's mother often bragged to her friends and family about how easy it was to care for her daughter. Thando was known for always being present and rarely speaking up. She had become skilled at being quiet, finding comfort in staying out of the spotlight, understanding the strength in her silence. Her mother admired that trait, seeing Thando's quiet nature as a sign of respect.

Pausing momentarily, Thando directed her gaze towards the neatly written poem on the chalkboard; she leaned forward, drawn in by the magnetic pull of the words. Her fingers gently traced the air, mimicking the script on the chalkboard, trying to capture the poem's essence; the repetition of the phrase "Hey, black Child" grabbed her attention. Her brow furrowed slightly, her focus interrupted by a flashing neon sign outside the window that read 'Piggy's Tavern' in blue and pink colors. The tavern is open during school hours, with the cool kids walking in and out with beer bottles. In the distance, Thando saw the busy taxi rank busy with evening activity. She watched parents getting off taxis' grocery bags in hand.

Cars were a luxury few families could afford, and the local taxi bus was the preferred mode of transportation. The air was heavy with swirling smoke, a reminder of families kindling fires in their coal stoves. Through the smoky haze, Thando felt the responsibility settling on her young shoulders. With the evening drawing near, she knew it was time to run back home, leaving behind the laughter and freedom of her schoolyard.

Her mind was racing with all the things she needed to do. She was overwhelmed with her to-do list, especially the laundry. She needed to wash and iron her school clothes – just a couple of shirts and socks – so they'd be ready for tomorrow. Juggling the same few items all week was just part of her routine.

Peering out the window, she watched the popular kids hanging around the nearby tavern, sparking her curiosity. She daydreamed about her future – maybe she'd get a great job and build a big house, complete with a luxury she longed for, an indoor bathroom, as her friend had. Or perhaps, even a giant dollhouse where she and her friends could have sleepovers. The thought brought a smile to her face. Then the school bell rang, snapping her back to reality. The streets were alive with kids heading home, them

laughter mingling with the tantalizing aroma of food. Thando knew she had to hurry. She had chores to finish and dinner to prepare before her mom returned home.

*

Thando's childhood was a constant juggle of emotions and obstacles. Every morning, she found comfort in the bustling activity of her neighborhood, where the sounds of daily life filled her room, instilling within her a profound sense of belonging. Not realizing it, she absorbed the vibe of her community, which left an imprint on her thoughts and personality.

Thando quietly observed the wisdom of her elders, who passed down their beliefs and values with each conversation. Behind their smiles and nods at family gatherings, she felt an invisible weight of expectations.

On special occasions, Thando's parents would whisk her away to the city, where her eyes were immediately drawn to the towering billboards that dominated the bustling streets. Faces that mirrored her own stared back at her. They were devoid of the depth and uniqueness that defined her identity. It felt as though her culture and heritage had been commodified, reduced to mere caricatures for mass consumption.

In contrast to the vibrant tapestry of her Zulu heritage, renowned for its intricate colorful beadwork and multifaceted traditions, the city's portrayal stood in total contrast. Here, diversity seemed commercialized, a mere shallow imitation that lacked the depth and authenticity resonating with Thando's soul. The skillfully crafted beadwork and the vivid beauty of traditional fabrics were reduced to a spectacle for entertainment, failing to capture the true essence of her people's culture.

After their city trips. They would ride back in a taxi, the fading sunlight seemed to amplify the shadows of hardship that loomed over their community. Thando and her family would walk through their neighborhood, where the effects of long-standing poverty were evident. The tired buildings mirrored the struggles of the people who called them home.

It felt like poverty had cast a heavy cloud over their aspirations, making it challenging to keep hope alive. Each day seemed like a battle against the odds, with little room for optimism in the face of such adversity.

As time flowed on, Thando's discomfort with her surroundings deepened, a subtle dissonance in the township's rhythm tugging at her five senses without revealing its source. She found comfort in the community's shared experience, knowing she wasn't alone in her unease. The communal sentiment echoed in her friend, Lala

Mahlangu by birth but forever known by her childhood nickname, a testament to the innocence that persisted into adulthood.

Like Thando, Lala cared about societal expectations and labels. In their community, individuals were often defined by their actions. Forever marked by the impressions they left behind. Their neighbor, Mlilo, whose name, meaning "fire," hinted at the chaotic force she once caused. As a child, Mlilo would mischievously set fires in the nearby fields. A spectacle that created great panic among the neighbors. Her behavior became a defining trait stamped into their collective memory.

Thando had never been given a nickname, it was as if the world had already labeled her with one: "Ugly and Invisible." Hurtful comments from society about her dark skin and unique features replayed in her mind over and over. She lived in a world where beauty was a privilege exclusively reserved for those with fairer complexions, making her feel like an outsider in her skin. Even though everyone in her community was black, there appeared to be a noticeable difference in skin tones.

Her perception was shaped one afternoon by an incident she witnessed from her window. A sudden commotion outside caught Thando's attention: her neighbor, known for her commanding voice, was scolding a young troublemaker for throwing rocks at her roof. 'Your light skin is the reason you can't behave, isn't it?' the neighbor yelled, her voice a blend of frustration and conviction, directed at the light-skinned boy. 'Maybe you should go live with your father in the mines!' she continued, her tone escalating with anger. The incident, coupled with the neighbor's harsh remarks, led Thando to believe that those with lighter skin must be from exotic, foreign lands, their mysterious origins contributing to their intriguing beauty.

Growing up, Thando longed for acceptance and yearned for someone to see beyond the surface, to recognize the radiance inside her. The mirror became a harsh stage where the clash between society's strict demands and Thando's strong desire for self-acceptance played out relentlessly.

In moments of self-doubt, Lala became a captivating source of inspiration, activating a dormant passion within Thando. Lala possessed an enchanting charm with her prominent cheekbones and smooth, dark chocolate complexion that radiated confidence. Her long, straight black hair represented elegance, a rare and precious quality in a world that often-imposed narrow beauty standards on black girls.

Thando's fingers often tangled in her hair, its coarse texture, whispered tales of insecurities. Through the lens of admiration, she saw Lala as the embodiment of grace and strength.

Even though they looked aesthetically different, they shared a common disdain for the shade of their skin. The cruel taunts from their peers about being too dark haunted them. Thando and Lala carried the weight of those hurtful words.

On one of the scorching hot afternoons, Lala's mind sparked an audacious idea—a plan she believed would finally liberate them from their predicament.

Lala had often watched her grandmother skillfully eliminate stubborn black stains from pristine white school shirts. With a bottle of Jik and a dash of Handy Andy, her grandmother seemed to work magic, making the black stains vanish as if they never existed. The process filled Lala with awe and hope, as she saw the potential of those cleaning products to bring about a brighter future and make their dreams come true. To her, it felt like a hidden miracle waiting to be unveiled, as if the solution to their torment and struggles was within reach, waiting for them to seize it.

During Miss. Dube's English lesson, Lala leaned close to Thando, her voice filled with vigor. "Thando, I know what can help us so other kids can stop teasing us," she whispered, nudging her to ensure she was paying attention. "It's like the Jik and Handy Andy stuff. You know how they make white clothes clean by magic? Well, maybe they can do something cool for us too, like making our skin a bit lighter."

When Lala mentioned the transformative potential of Jik and Handy Andy, Thando's eyes widened with curiosity, contemplating the possibilities. My grandma always uses OMO soap. Can that soap make our skin amazing".

Doubts crept into her mind, questioning whether these seemingly extravagant brands could live up to their claims.

Albeit the uncertainty, a glimmer of hope flickered within Thando. The idea of finding a solution to their struggles was too enticing to ignore. With conviction, Lala replied, her voice brimming with excitement, "I pinkie swear; they will work."

They ventured to the local shop, located a few streets away from their school, the vibrant colors of its signage caught their attention. The Spaza Shop was a modest, single-story building with a corrugated metal roof. It stood between a row of similar small businesses, with the outside walls covered with posters of hair products, household essentials, and beverages. The shop was compact, and efficiently organized to maximize the available space. Narrow aisles were lined with neatly arranged shelves, stocked with different products. They could hear the soft hum of the refrigerators and the shuffle of footsteps as other customers browsed the shop. The friendly shopkeeper welcomed them with a warm smile, putting them at ease immediately.

They started their search; their hearts were filled with excitement. They knew that somewhere among those shelves were the ingredients for a plan that could completely change their lives. With excitement and panic, they paid for their purchases, their minds already racing with ideas and possibilities.

Outside the Spaza shop, the sun cast its warm glow upon the bustling streets of their neighborhood. The world seemed to hold its breath, waiting to witness the outcome of the secret pact they had made.

They arrived at Lala's house and nervously exchanged glances with her grandmother, who seemed preoccupied with her brothers and cousins. A spark of hope set off in their hearts. That was their chance to transform, away from prying eyes and without any disturbances.

In the bathroom, they locked away their fears and sealed the windows for privacy. The air was thick with the strong smell of bleach and the refreshing scent of lemon from the detergent. It felt suffocating and exciting at the same time. They coughed uncontrollably and after a while, the coughing stopped, and they composed themselves. They stepped into the water, armed with scrubbing brushes. With each stroke, they hoped the bleach and detergent would wash away their physical appearance along with the doubts and insecurities that troubled them for so long.

The water turned murky as they scrubbed away the layers they wanted to shed. The bathroom walls seemed to witness their efforts, echoing their strong desire for change. With every stroke, they wished for their blemishes and imperfections to disappear, leaving behind only the perfect image they longed for.

They stepped out of the water toweling themselves dry, the disappointment in Lala's eyes was evident.

"Is there any change? Do you see it?" she asked, her voice tinged with desperation, trying to soothe the persistent burning sensation on her irritated skin. Thando's heart sank, knowing that their transformation hadn't manifested in the way they had hoped. With towels wrapped around their bodies, they gazed at each other, their reflections showing no significant difference in their appearances.

Thando analyzed Lala's reflection; she felt her heart soften. "Uhm, your skin looks kinda pink, but the towel is still all clean, and there aren't any black marks." there was no noticeable physical change, an Unsaid understanding passed between them.

They sat on the floor in silence, their eyes locked, raised eyebrow from one was met with a subtle nod from the other, and in that silent connection. A world of inferred thoughts passed between them, reminding each other of the consequences that lurked outside the bathroom door. The throbbing skin brought Thando's attention back to her body, with the cold towel pressed against her aching legs. It was clear to both of them in that moment of discomfort that they could not change their skin color. It was part of who they were.

Thando said her goodbyes and left Lala's house that fateful Thursday afternoon, a blend of emotions swept over her. The lingering scent of detergents clung to her clothes, serving as a poignant reminder of their failed attempt to alter their appearances. With every gentle breeze that caressed her neck, she felt a twinge of pain, a bittersweet reminder of the world's judgment and the weight of society's expectations.

Without realizing it, she confronted her judgments and that of society's narrow standards of beauty. She understood that her skin tone might not be hailed as conventionally attractive.

Their lives carried on, and Thando and Lala continued their journey, their friendship evolving into a strong and unbreakable bond. They shared a secret understanding that transcended words, a connection forged by the shared struggles they faced. While the world around them remained oblivious to the battles they fought within themselves, their hearts yearned for self-acceptance and belonging.

*

Thando's entry into puberty stirred deep emotions, mirroring the winds of transformation sweeping through her township. Her journey paralleled the change sweeping through her township. Just as her body transformed, with her hips slowly widening hugging her jeans and her T-shirts stretching slightly across her chest, accommodating her growing breast, her community was also experiencing a shift, triggering a vortex of emotions and reactions among its residents.

A growing awareness of self-made her conscious of how others perceived her. Her dark skin glowed, and she began experimenting with makeup, straddling the line between staying true to her cultural heritage and adopting modern trends. She took on bold lip colors and vivid eyeshadows became her artistic tools, allowing her to express her emerging individuality.

Her traditional attire and modern influences clashed, and the township expressed the crossroads.

Urbanization gathered momentum; its undeniable force reshaped the landscape. The ruling government of that era keenly grasped the growing discontent among the populace inhabiting the townships. The desire to no longer remain secluded within desolate enclaves was palpable. The people's aspirations had evolved; they thirsted to actively engage on the global stage and tap into the potential of technological advancements. Denying them the chance would inevitably sow the seeds of further political unrest, a storm hovering on the horizon.

During the current uncertainty, a glimmer of hope emerged – the promise of progress and uncharted vistas. The neighborhood Thando knew so well was transforming right before his eyes. Modern skyscrapers and bustling new businesses were popping up everywhere, overshadowing the small houses and old markets that had been the heart of the community for so long. Watching these giant buildings rise, Thando was struck by the tug-of-war between the cherished old ways and the exciting possibilities of a new era.

The landscape rapidly evolved, and a clear distinction emerged between those who embraced the advancements and those struggling to adapt. While some eagerly welcomed urbanization, others clung tightly to cherished traditions. The growing divide between the haves and the have-nots became more apparent each day. New businesses flourished, attracting the promise of a better life for some, while others were left behind, unable to keep up with the pace of change.

Puberty brought with it a rollercoaster of physical and emotional changes, and she navigated the challenges of adolescence while trying to understand her place in the evolving world. With the shifting tide, Thando's family remained trapped in poverty, with their circumstances unchanged while the new developments around them were flourishing. Seeing her mother work tirelessly to make ends meet, especially when it came to affording necessities like sanitary towels, filled Thando with concern and responsibility. The changes in the town did not lessen their financial burden, and the promise of progress seemed distant for her family.

Nothing within her immediate reality pointed to a brighter future.

Looking for comfort, she turned inward, taking permanent residence in her room, a cocoon of solitude where the noise of the outside world was silenced. It was in the solace space that she allowed her wildest thoughts to roam free. Deep in her mind, she wrestled with the audacity of hope, questioning whether it was even possible for someone like her—a black child living in a world where societal norms and prejudice seemed to dictate her future. The poem that spoke of hope and possibility felt foreign to her reality, making her question if her dreams were even possible for a black child like her.

I. THE KEYS TO SUCCESS

In a world where having money meant being happy, Thando's parents had a simple plan for success. "Go to school, get your degree, and find a well-paying job." Their advice was about something other than making money. It came from a need to survive, working hard to maintain the modest four-bedroom house they called home.

Thando admired her parents' dedication and sacrifices, knowing they were their household's backbone. Her mother, a diligent hotel cleaner, and her father, a dedicated bus driver, understood the value of hard work and the importance of earning every penny they could.

The family had faced difficult times before when her father lost his job twice. The first setback was because of a mysterious downturn in the bus company's fortunes, leading to an unthinkable number of people getting laid off. Irrespective of facing many difficulties, he found a new job, which felt like a small achievement in the face of constant challenges. Things took a turn for the worse when he had a big argument with his close coworker, Vusi, who had since become a family friend and a dear uncle to Thando.

Sneaky rumours were swirling in the community, hinting at an alleged affair between Thando's father and Uncle Vusi's wife—a topic strictly forbidden within the walls of their home, causing a lot of tension. Complex emotions boiled, and Uncle Vusi's pride was wounded. He wanted payback. He planted illegal drugs in Thando's dad's bus, intending to anonymously tip off the authorities. The scheme worked, and when the illicit substances were discovered on the bus, it caused a severe blow to his credibility as a bus driver. The company had no choice; they had to dismiss him immediately, leaving him jobless and shamed.

*

For Thando's parents, success meant more than just financial stability; it meant having enough money to care for their needs and breaking free from the constant worry of not having enough. Their dreams of a better life were deeply rooted in the belief that education held the key to fulfillment and prosperity. They projected these aspirations onto Thando, hoping she would grasp the elusive concept of using education as a magical key to unlock her potential and create a brighter future for herself and their family.

Thando observed how her mother's expectations evolved as the years passed. It was in the subtle nuances of her mother's conversations, the additional books placed on the shelves, and the newfound emphasis on Thando's intellectual growth. Her mother's expectations for her exceeded what their immediate community demanded of her. It went further to include exploring and learning new things about herself.

Her mother had reimagined her dreams for Thando, quietly steering away from the traditional path. Thando's role was to be a wife and caretaker, encouraging her to be educated and emancipated.

Her mother's relentless push for formal education echoed in her ears; it was as if her mother's new goals had occupied her thoughts, and a friendly and insistent neighbour was dropping by uninvited. The onus of those words was undeniable, gently nudging her toward the road her mother believed she should travel.

*

When the time came for Thando to head to university, her family left no stone unturned in evaluating each university option. With finances stretched thin, the stakes were high, and they couldn't risk a hasty decision. Night after night, they gathered around the kitchen table, a chaos of papers in front of them, analysing the tuition costs, scholarship possibilities, and potential living expenses. Thando's mother, having reimagined a brighter future for her daughter, was mainly focused on ensuring Thando could attend a well-regarded, affordable university. Each school was meticulously discussed, its merits and disadvantages carefully balanced against their financial realities.

Their home, peeling and needing paint, was filled with a vital air of purpose. They managed their tight budget while still caring for everyday needs, always ready to make sacrifices for Thando's education.

After many discussions, she decided to attend a nearby university and live at home.

*

Her peers revelled in the excitement of parties and social clubs during their university years. There was a quiet, oh-so-persistent case of Fear Of Missing Out tugging at Thando's heartstrings. Coming from different cities and towns to study, her new classmates embraced the thrill of new surroundings, immersing themselves in diverse cultures, food, and languages. Thando's world remained focused and routine on her studies and household responsibilities.

Thando couldn't resist wondering what it would be like to be part of those carefree gatherings, to let loose and dance the night away without the weight of responsibilities tugging at her conscience.

Thando would watch those carefree parties from afar and daydream like crazy. She'd imagine herself dancing away until sunrise, not a single worry on her mind. They all came from different backgrounds, each friend bringing a unique thread to the university experience.

She would sometimes scroll through social media, seeing her friends' posts filled with laughter and adventure, and the FOMO intensified. The desire to break free from the library's confines, to experience life in its most unscripted form, was an ever-present ache within her.

Thando couldn't allow herself to be swayed by those fleeting desires. Though she never directly asked her new friends about their family dynamic, it was evident that the weight of family obligations didn't seem to rest as heavily on their shoulders as it did on hers. At the very least, they didn't let it bother them.

*

"Two Bs don't mix," her mother's words echoed through Thando's mind like a booming drumbeat, their meaning etched deep into her soul. "Boys and Books don't go together," her mother would repeat, each word dripping with resolve, her steady gaze piercing Thando's very being. The statement didn't follow the standard rules of language; its weighty significance reverberated within Thando—it was a commandment, a warning that education must always come first. It became a relentless chant, beating through the chambers of her heart, compelling her to discard any distractions or barriers that could hinder her relentless pursuit of knowledge.

Thando got used to life on campus, and every day brought something new. She loved watching students hang out and laugh together on the grass, a sight that had become a regular part of her day. One normal day suddenly became unforgettable when she noticed someone who stood out from the crowd.

Thando couldn't help but notice the striking presence of a tall, handsomely built man on campus. His smooth, cocoa-coloured skin seemed almost edible, perfectly complemented by the curve of his lips, which held a charming smile at the corners. He exuded confidence in every step as if he had secrets known only to him. She couldn't take her eyes off him.

Then, suddenly, Micheal stopped and turned around sharply, sensing Thando's gaze on him. Their eyes met, and Thando felt a rush of warmth. Her heart skipped a beat with the excitement of the unexpected moment. Thando quickly ducked into the university bookshop, her thoughts swirling chaotically from that intense moment. '*What's wrong with you Thando. That was so embarrassing* she muttered, her cheeks burning with humiliation?' '*Why am I sweating?*' she muttered, fanning herself as she unbuttoned the top of her shirt dress for cool air. She looked down and noticed her damp bra; she sighed in relief.

Looking up, Thando's heart skipped a beat. Micheal, wearing a pair of white designer sneakers, was tall, his dark eyes twinkling, and he had a broad smile. Thando's breath caught in her throat as she realized he was right there, just a few feet away.

From their serendipitous meeting in the bookshop, Thando and Micheal, an older man pursuing his master's part-time, were swept up in a whirlwind romance. Disregarding the 18-year age gap, they were inseparable, sharing countless hours. With his mature outlook and part-time student status, Micheal brought a different perspective that fascinated Thando.

They would spend time under the oak trees on campus, and their conversations would drift from academic challenges to personal dreams and aspirations. On weekends, Michael would whisk Thando away to explore the city, introducing her to secluded hotels and restaurants she had never imagined visiting or even heard of. Financially stable, he spared no expense.

Although they cherished their time together, Micheal often had to travel for work, preventing them from spending entire weekends together. His frequent absences also meant he couldn't meet Thando's friends, making it difficult for Thando to share her excitement about her newfound love with her family and friends.

*

Thando was hooked on Micheal's charm when whispers that he was happily married began circulating on campus, contradicting his stories of separation and his claims that his wife was stubbornly clinging to their failed marriage. In defiance of the mounting doubts, Thando hesitated to confront him. Instead, she chose to stay in the relationship, holding onto the hope that he would eventually leave his wife as he promised. She didn't want to seem childish or prone to gossip. The information should have served as a deterrent, a warning sign to retreat. However, Micheal's charm, an intangible magnetism that defied reason, captivated her.

"He's the first man who makes me feel both beautiful and confident," Thando confided in Lala, sitting in the cozy corner of their Favorite café. Lala, who had witnessed Thando's remarkable transformation over the years, nodded in understanding.

"You've come into your own lately," Lala remarked, seeing how Thando was glowing in love.

Thando smiled gratefully. "It's like a silent revolution within me," she explained, sipping her drink thoughtfully. "And with Micheal, I've stepped into a whole new world. He's not just a companion; he's a delicious e of emotions I've never experienced."

Lala leaned in, intrigued. "Tell me more. What's he like?"

Thando's face lit up as she recounted her adventures with Micheal, describing each moment as if it were a scene from a movie. "Every time we're together, it's like escaping into an alternate reality," she said, her voice filled with wonder. "He's shown me a life of luxury and opulence that I never even knew existed outside of magazines."

Thando, at the brink of 18, found herself drawn by Micheal's unmistakable confidence and authority. Aged 38, he possessed a wisdom and self-control that seemed monumental compared to the youthful exuberance of her peers. The contrast was obvious against the backdrop of her father, who, after losing his job, surrendered to despair and alcohol, losing all shadow of manly authority in Thando's eyes.

Micheal's mastery over his life and masculinity deeply intrigued Thando, setting him apart in her eyes. Yet, with her growing interest, she realized she could only offer vague answers when her friends inquired about him. The most compelling aspect of Micheal was the enigmatic aura that enveloped him, a mystery that kept Thando perennially engaged and slightly out of reach. She hung on every word he spoke, swallowing his stories whole without a trace of scepticism.

Usually, one to uphold her mother's rules strictly, Thando was irresistibly drawn into an unexpected affair, falling in love with an older, married man.

Thando discovered a newfound energy and zest for life during those stolen moments with Micheal. Everything else faded; her friends and studies took a backseat. She got lost in the attractive things her new life offered.

She temporarily escaped her money troubles and basked in the thrill of having it all. The happiness from having fancy things and the strong pull of a limitless love was like something out of her dreams.

As a reaction to being acknowledged and appreciated, Thando gave herself to Micheal completely, both mentally and physically, without any reservations. Her secret relationship with Micheal made her feel noticed and deeply cared for.

*

In her final year of studies, she eagerly anticipates her upcoming graduation. Exhaustion weighed her down, making her mind foggy and sluggish. Days before her final exam, Thando felt overwhelmed by the stress of upcoming exams, making it hard to notice the subtle changes in her body. The fatigue and queasiness became too much to bear, and she decided to visit the University clinic to get a sick note that could give her a valid excuse for her upcoming exam.

During the exam, the room was dead quiet except for the loud pounding of Thando's heart in her ears. It was cold and smelled faintly of disinfectant, adding to her nervousness. The doctor looked at the nurses, their expressions full of worry and surprise. When they finally said, "You are pregnant," it hit Thando like a ton of bricks.

She caught her breath and gripped the edge of the exam table tightly.

Everything around her seemed to blur, including the medical tools on a tray nearby.

Seeing how upset she was, the doctor touched her arm gently. "Thando, are you alright? Do you need a moment?" his voice was kind and calming in the chilly room. The nurse could not be bothered and made a sarcastic remark, "Another one? Seems like we get a student in here every week pretending they don't know how these things happen." Her tone was light and carried a sharp edge, clashing with the doctor's kindness.

Thando was barely listening. Her mind was elsewhere, caught up in memories of Micheal and their secret times together, and now, facing the natural consequences of their relationship. The thought that everything in her life was about to change completely sent a shiver through her face. She nodded slowly; her voice stuck in her throat.

*

Thando stood in the living room, her heart pounding like a drum. She took a deep breath, trying her best to calm herself. Her mother was sitting on the couch, routinely reviewing all the post-box mail she had collected in the week.

"Mum," Thando began, her voice a little shaky. There's something I need to talk to you about." Her mother looked away from what she was doing, curious and startled by Thado's serious tone.

Thando talked about what was on her mind, detailing her relationship with Michael and the news she received from the nurse at the University clinic. Every word she spoke seemed to build a wall between them, made of hurt and disappointment. She knew her mother might not react well, and she was not ready for what came next.

"Who is this person, Thando?

Thando's fingers fidgeted with the edge of her shirt, her gaze darting to the floor before meeting her mother's eyes again. "His name is Micheal, and he's... he's married." the room's atmosphere grew heavier. Each word Thando spoke was a brick in an invisible wall between them, a divide fuelled by anger and disappointment.

"Thando, you know that's not right" " her mother's voice was calm and deep with disappointment. And those were the last words she spoke on the news of the pregnancy.

The room, once a safe place, felt strange and distant, full of broken dreams. The quiet that followed felt heavy, a reminder of the gap that had grown between them.

Thando went to her room, tears filling her eyes. Through the thin walls, she could hear her mother crying, too, a sad reminder of the pain they were both going through. The home that used to be warm and comforting felt cold and empty.

*

Graduating wasn't just a goal—it was a lifeline for her and her unborn child, something she clung to with unwavering determination. It wasn't just about getting a diploma but securing a brighter future for herself and her little one. Every assignment and exam was a step closer to stability and opportunity. Her inner whisper said *'I've failed myself, but I won't fail this life inside of me too'.*

Thando stood before a large, eager crowd on her graduation day, wearing her graduation robe. It felt like the pinnacle of her academic journey, as her bachelor's degree in social studies symbolized her countless hours poring over textbooks.

The atmosphere was electric. Everywhere Thando looked, groups of people clapped each other on the back, raising glasses in toast and sharing happy smiles over their accomplishments. Balloons bobbed against the ceiling, and confetti sprinkled the floor, adding to the festive atmosphere. Amongst the cheers and applause, there was an undercurrent of tension that Thando couldn't ignore.

She caught herself scanning the crowd, her eyes briefly searching for Micheal, knowing he was in the crowd with his family. She quickly redirected her focus back to the ceremony. That was her time to celebrate her academic success. Even so, she couldn't ignore the vulnerability that nibbled at her heart.

Her black graduation robe, meant to symbolize her academic journey, felt more like a veil. Underneath, it hid the deep shame she carried.

She walked confidently across the stage, her heart pounding with excitement and nervousness. That was her moment to shine, her moment to be celebrated. As she made her way to the centre to receive her degree in Social Studies, the applause grew louder, and she could see proud faces beaming at her from the audience. She soaked in the warmth of their admiration, her steps measured and sure.

Halfway across the stage, a sudden, cold, and chilling sensation trickled down her legs, seeping into the fabric of her gown. Her face flushed with embarrassment, and her hands trembled as she maintained her composure. Each step became a monumental effort as she tried to gracefully reach the other side of the stage, desperately hoping to conceal the mishap beneath her gown.

Thando excused herself, desperate to escape the curious eyes that seemed to follow her every move. She hurried to the bathroom for privacy. She locked the door behind her while excruciating pain tore through her body, and a rush of blood spilled onto the floor, staining her clean white high heels. The walls of the bathroom seemed to close in on her, suffocating her under the weight of her horrifying reality. Panic stopped her heart, sending fear and desperation coursing through her veins. With trembling hands, she grabbed at every piece of paper within reach, frantically trying to wipe away the blood that marked her as a bearer of loss and sorrow. Despite her efforts to scrub away the traces, she couldn't erase the pain and sorrow that swept over her soul.

The bathroom floor transformed into a canvas of tragedy streaked with blood that narrated a tale Thando wished she could keep to herself. Leaning against the cold tile, her mind was filled with questions and regrets. "Why did this happen? Was it something I did? Could I have prevented it?" The guilt weighed heavily on her, each thought amplifying the pain and anguish of her miscarriage.

For long minutes, Thando remained alone, grappling with her sadness. No one knew what had happened; she hadn't called anyone, unsure what to say or how to explain. Finally, gathering her strength, she cleaned herself up as best she could, wiping the floor in a futile attempt to erase the evidence of her loss. She checked her reflection in the mirror, wiped away her tears, and forced a smile onto her face.

Waddling out of the bathroom, Thando rejoined her graduation celebration, hiding her pain behind a mask of joy. She knew she couldn't burden her friends and family with her sorrow, not on that day.

Thando looked across the room as if playing a cruel joke on her. Micheal, the very root of her recent heartache, was holding his daughter snugly in his arms while his wife stood beside him, radiating pride. They looked like the perfect family portrait, and it twisted a knife in her already aching heart.

The celebration around her continued unabated, filled with laughter and cheerful applause. She did her best to blend into the festive atmosphere, her heart still loaded with loss and grief.

*

After Thando's graduation, a heavy and solemn silence settled between her and her mother. They never spoke about the incident or Thando's pregnancy. The barrier of unspoken words stood between them, creating an invisible barrier neither could cross. For her mother, the day had been about celebrating her daughter's achievement, a joyous occasion that she believed should overshadow personal troubles.

Back at home, another secret took residence in the walls of their house, teetering on the brink of revelation yet restrained by their mutual discomfort. The walls of their home yet again bore silent witness to their struggles, absorbing the tension and safeguarding their hidden truths. Both Thando and her mother felt the heaviness of the fact they couldn't bring themselves to speak about it.

Each day, they struggled silently, unable to muster the courage to shatter the fragile peace with the painful realities that had stained their relationship.

Thando's wounds had not healed with time; instead, they festered, giving off the haunting odour of shame from her graduation day. She was ag to find a job. A constant reminder of the financial burden it had put on her parents, pushing her towards a determined resolve to find a job.

She spent long hours at the local internet cafe next to the neighbourhood shop. It was a smelly, crowded place, where the aroma of stale coffee mixed with the scent of sweat from strangers hunched over their screens, each lost in their online activities.

Thando arrived early at "Big Daddy's Internet Cafe" every day and settled into the creaky plastic chairs and worn-out tables. The noise of computers humming and people chatting added to the cafe's atmosphere. Through the clamour, she honed in on her computer screen, which became her gateway to a world of job opportunities beyond Big Daddy's Internet cafe.

Thando's fingers moved steadily over the keyboard as she navigated job portals, company websites, and online forums. She went through each listing and submitted over 30 applications. Each click became a routine.

*

On a regular Tuesday at the internet cafe, Thando was sifting through her emails, her expectations tempered by the familiar sting of past rejections. She paused when she saw a new notification, her instinct to brace for another disappointment almost automatic. With a resigned click, she opened the email.

Earlier that morning, her mother had woken up in a terrible mood; the tension was hard to escape in their small home. Feeling the need to escape and find some peace, Thando decided Big

Daddy's Internet Cafe was a familiar place where she could focus on the future and, hopefully, make some progress in her job search. As she sat in the crowded, noisy room, the hum of conversation and clicking of keyboards around her, Thando found a moment of consolation in her job-hunting routine, away from the stress at home.

To her surprise, the subject line read: "Congratulations! Internship Offer Inside!" The news slowly registered as Thando read and reread the email. Despite her academic background in social studies, which is different from the finance field, she landed an internship at one of the city's most prestigious finance firms.

. It was the last place she expected to succeed. The finance sector was notorious for favouring candidates with degrees in economics or business. Opportunities were fiercely competitive, often going to students from the top universities with more 'relevant' majors. Although she would be working in the social department of the company, a division more aligned with her studies in social studies, she was excited to get a place in a competitive industry.

She spent another fifteen minutes gazing at the screen, soaking in every word of the offer. Thando quickly gathered her things, her movements brisk and purposeful. She logged off the computer, barely noticing the usual sounds of the cafe, and jogged home. She burst through the door, calling out to her mother with an enthusiasm she couldn't contain. "Mom, you won't believe what happened!" she exclaimed, the news tumbling out before her mother could even thoroughly look up from her chores. Her infectious excitement filled the small space with a new, hopeful energy.

At that moment, she felt a surge of gratitude. Although the opportunity might not have been the full-time job she initially hoped for, it was a step in the right direction.

Thando, twenty-one years old at the start of the job and without any debt, did not frown at the year-long contract. Although the pay was low—barely covering her transportation and lunch costs—there was a possibility of an extension if she delivered exceptional results.". The pay was low, barely enough to cover her transportation and lunch costs. She was 21 and had not amassed any debt, yet there was a possibility of an extension if she managed to deliver exceptional results. However, Thando didn't dwell on that possibility. She accepted the contract conditions and embraced the flow of events, considering the natural course of progression. She accepted the job without complaints and followed the established path, not questioning where it might lead.

The first four months of her internship raced by, with a demanding induction program and the challenge of enrolling for a postgraduate degree. She felt overwhelmed. Just when adjusting to her new routine, she was assigned to another department to work closely with a senior manager in the finance department. The position allowed Thando to apply her robust analytical skills, evaluate financial data, and forecast future trends.

Her natural talent for numbers made her the perfect fit for the role. Thando loved the meaningful work she was doing, which not only impressed her managers but also resonated with the entire team.

Thando quickly earned praise for her ability to make complex financial data easy to understand. Her team valued her knack for translating detailed numbers into practical strategies. Her work directly influenced the team's operations, which was a big change from her background in social studies. The newly discovered purpose brought a deep fulfillment and confidence that was entirely new to her.

Thando often grappled with the company's tricky financial data as an intern. She knew how to break down complex problems into simpler terms that even those not versed in Finance could understand. She leaned on what she already knew, improving each task, which gave her a sense of achievement. It was like starting a new, exciting book chapter—each day brought new challenges and chances to show what she could do.

Every Monday, Thando stood before her colleagues in the dimly lit boardroom, presenting the latest customer data to summarize the week. These "Sh*t Data Dive Mondays." were a regular part of her internship, and while she was nervous at first, she gradually grew more comfortable speaking up. The team welcomed her, acknowledging her effort and her clarity on complex information.

*

On the last Monday of her contract, Thando arrived early at the meeting room to meet with her hiring manager, Dennis. Sunlight streamed through the window, brightening the space. As she waited, her thoughts drifted back to the start of her internship—struggling with complex math problems and wrestling with stacks of paperwork. Reflecting on her journey, she could see the growth in her skills and felt proud of her achievements, knowing her mom was too.

"Consider a career in Finance," Dennis commanded, reclining in his chair, his gaze fixed on Thando.

She managed a faint smile and responded, "Me? You mean continue working in this bank?"

"Not exactly," Dennis replied, crossing his legs, and leaning forward. "I wish we could offer you a permanent position here, but unfortunately, our internship program is being discontinued because of budget issues; I strongly encourage you to explore a career in Finance. Your talent with numbers is truly exceptional."

"I'll consider that," Thando replied softly, her mind spinning with conflicting emotions.

On one hand, she was praised for her skills, but on the other hand, she was faced with the possibility of losing her job.

The compliment felt bittersweet, like rough sandpaper against her skin. She trusted Dennis and developed a respectful working relationship. He was the first person to genuinely appreciate her work and value her opinions. Unlike Micheal, he did not try to sleep with her.

"You really should," Dennis insisted, his gratitude evident as he touched her shoulder.

"You've saved this department millions of dollars and countless hours. Your ability to simplify even the most complex formulas never fails to amaze me."

"Thank you, Dennis. I appreciate your recognition," she replied, a faint smile curving her lips, hinting at playful modesty.

Thando accepted Dennis's words without scepticism, welcoming them as genuine encouragement and a new perspective on her abilities. The revelation that she could pursue a career in Finance sparked excitement within her.

*

Thando approached her new position with a newfound energy of confidence and experience gained from her internship. After months of tireless searching and sending out countless job applications, she had finally secured the perfect entry-level position as a financial analyst at a rapidly growing startup in the financial industry. The refreshing winds of change swept through her work life, filling her with hope and anticipation for what lay ahead.

The company was smaller and less well-known than the high-profile firm where she had interned before. However, there was something special about the new place—it had a lively, dynamic energy that instantly clicked with her. The startup was making waves by creating innovative online products aimed at young people, much like Thando herself. It was the kind of fresh, creative environment she was looking for.

What made the opportunity stand out for her was the offer of a permanent contract.

She would no longer live in fear of losing her job at any moment. The promise of a stable position was priceless to her, and it made her smile every time she thought about it.

With the ink still fresh on her contract, Thando was excited about the possibilities ahead. She viewed the job as an opportunity for personal growth and professional development. In the dynamic startup environment, she would have the chance to learn and tackle new challenges—opportunities that might take years to handle in a large corporation like her previous one.

The role came with a welcome pay increase, supporting her plans to move to the city in the coming months—a dream she had nurtured for quite some time. It was the typical path, the unspoken trajectory followed by many: to leave the township as quickly as possible and return only for visits, often just to showcase fancy cars and parade in chic city attire. All her cousins had done the same, their departures transforming into tales of triumph that their mothers recounted with glowing pride. Thando was poised to follow the well-trodden path. The idea would be burst by a sting of embarrassment for wanting to abandon her community.

Days melded into weeks, and weeks revealed the months; Thando submerged herself deeply into her work, taking every opportunity to learn and grow. The once unfamiliar terrain of her new role gradually transformed into a sanctuary of comfort and confidence. She mastered her surroundings, turning initial overwhelm into familiarity. In the ebb and flow of the startup's culture, Thando learned to adapt and find her balance. Life.

*

Craig, her astute new manager, quickly noticed Thando's rapid learning pace and decided to accelerate her integration into the company. To facilitate her learning, he paired Thando with Allison, a seasoned Senior Financial Analyst renowned for her strict and effective mentoring style. Craig believed that Allison's expertise and wealth of experience would be ideal in helping Thando master the company's newly implemented IT system.

Over the first few days, Allison and Thando worked closely to sketch a detailed training plan. Thando was eager and full of questions, demonstrating her ambition to climb the corporate ladder. They delved deeper into the system's intricacies, and Thando's enthusiasm was met with Allison's precise, methodical guidance. However, during the busy flow of training sessions and shared ambitions, Thando began to pick up on subtle cues in Allison's behaviour—hints of undisclosed intentions that seemed to lurk beneath her mentor's composed exterior.

Thando noticed that Allison often steered her towards specific projects and away from others, whispering advice that seemed tactically charged, suggesting there might be more at play than professional grooming. Allison craftily took advantage of the situation to offload her unwanted administrative tasks onto Thando. She inundated her with paperwork and menial assignments, drowning Thando in trivial responsibilities.

During one of their weekly one-on-one meetings, the atmosphere was tense. Thando, usually composed, was in the spotlight. She had inadvertently failed to complete a task that Craig had assigned to Allison during their team staff meeting. Her mentor and ramping buddy, Allison, confronted her about the oversight. Thando's nerves tingled, sensing the brewing storm.

"Why haven't you done it?" Allison's voice rang out, her frustration evident. Taking a deep breath, Thando held her ground and explained that she had understood the task to be Allison's responsibility, not hers. Allison's face turned crimson, her voice hoarse with anger, and filled the room with cold tension. Then, her tone turned sharp and biting. "You better just shut up and do as you are told, black girl!"

Sitting upright in the black leather chair across the room, Allison froze, realizing the gravity of her words. She looked confused, caught in a moment of internal conflict, unsure whether to apologize—which might admit guilt—or to continue exerting her authority.

Thando's heart sank, shocked by the harshness of Allison's words.

Allison, choosing authority, with a pointed finger aimed straight at Thando, continued her threats.

"I won't hesitate to have you fired," she snapped, her words punctuated by flecks of spit.

"And before you know it," her tone was unforgiving, "you'll be selling snacks at a street corner in the township!"

Allison's frustration echoed sharply through the boardroom as she slammed her notebook shut with enough force to make the table tremble and her water glass tip over. The decisive sound of the door slamming shut marked the abrupt end of the meeting, leaving Thando alone to contemplate the veiled threat and the bleak prospect of ending up as a humble street vendor at a busy township intersection.

Thando stood motionless; her feet anchored to the floor by invisible chains. Her body visibly tensed from the emotional turmoil, making her posture rigid. Her shoulders drooped slightly, burdened by unseen chains, while her arms hung listlessly at her sides. Her lips, usually curved in a gentle smile, were straight lines, silently broadcasting the deep disappointment that engulfed her.

Thando's mind raced, frantically searching her past experiences for anything that might match the profound sense of worthlessness engulfing her. No previous incident, not even her most embarrassing moments or the painful memory of a miscarriage on her graduation day, came close to the intensity of the emotions she felt in that confrontation with Allison.

The new emotion was uncharted territory for her. It was a dark hole that threatened to consume her self-worth.

She fought to contain her tears; her hands balled into tight fists—a physical manifestation of the turmoil swirling inside her.

*

Determined to prove Allison wrong and advance her career without compromise, Thando adopted a more assertive approach by changing her work routine. Embodying a strong black girl mindset, she devised a challenging new daily commute that allowed her to start her day earlier and stay later if necessary. She wanted to prove her commitment to not only meet but exceed expectations at work.

Her day started in the dark before the sun rose, and the birds filled the morning with their songs. She sat in a crowded taxi bus daily, surrounded by weary individuals on their way to uninspiring jobs. Looking around, she saw the defeated expressions on their faces, each telling a story of dreams slowly fading and still burdened with the heavy responsibility of providing for their families.

Facing the early mornings, Thando found strength in the words of Mr. Useni Eugene Perkins, which echoed in her mind:

"You can learn what you want to learn if you try to learn what you can."

The mantra helped her overcome the fear of facing the same fate as her fellow commuters. With a clear focus, she approached each day with a steadfast resolve, viewing every challenge as an opportunity to advance her career and overcome barriers.

Aware of chilling accounts from her black coworkers who had been fired and publicly shamed for voicing their grievances to HR, Thando recognized the real risk of being unfairly targeted and losing her job if she spoke out against Allison. Consequently, she chose not to report the incident, carrying an underlying anxiety that stifled her voice at work. She silently carried her daily struggles, viewing them not as burdens but as hurdles she needed to overcome to progress in her career.

Aware of the alarming stories from her fellow black coworkers who had been fired and publicly criticized for raising their concerns to H.R., Thando recognized the real risk of facing unfair consequences and potentially losing her job if she confronted Allison. Knowing how much her family relied on her to keep the job and her goals of buying a car and moving to the city, Thando felt that enduring Allison's behaviour was a necessary sacrifice.

With this awareness, she opted not to report the incident, a decision that introduced a profound, underlying anxiety that muted her voice at work. Thando silently managed her struggles each day, viewing them as essential challenges to navigate to advance in her career.

Disregarding the residual tension from the harsh boardroom confrontation, Thando saw it necessary to maintain a professional relationship with Allison. It placed a heavy emotional burden on her. Allison's harsh words had deeply impacted Thando, undermining her self-assurance.

"Do you know you can learn, what you want to learn if you try to learn, what you can learn?" Like a broken tape, Mr. Perkins's haunting words echoed relentlessly in her mind, their tone dripping with the bitter taste of defeat. The poet's voice, once an inspiration, served as a painful reminder of her perceived shortcomings.

Thando's pursuit of career advancement in the demanding finance industry meant late nights at the office and weekends spent studying and preparing for presentations. The schedule left her with few opportunities for social activities or maintaining any meaningful connections. Her professional commitments all her time and energy, leaving little room for a personal life.

Sitting in the bustling local salon, Thando watched the hairstylist skilfully wove vibrant strands of synthetic fiber into intricate, colourful braids. The rhythmic movements of the stylist's hands created a soothing backdrop to the lively atmosphere around her. Each braid—a blend of bold colours turquoise, magenta, wine red, and sunflower yellow—seemed to charge her with a silent strength while she viewed her transformation in the mirror. The moment of change resonated deeply with her, mirroring the internal shifts she felt and contemplating her career.

Under the salon's glaring lights, surrounded by the laughter and chatter of other customers, Thando felt at home. She settled into the comfortable hum of the salon; a sobering thought crossed her mind. *When David suggested I pursue a career in this industry, he left out a few details*—that the industry was dominated by Caucasian alpha males, many of whom had credentials from prestigious business schools, she had never heard of. She felt an absolute disconnect, perceiving herself as lacking the necessary tools to achieve a successful career. Her unrealized potential pressed heavily upon her, intensified by the traumatic experience with Allison, which had shaken her confidence and muted her voice. Under the salon's glaring lights, amidst the laughter and chatter of other patrons.

While the hair stylist skilfully chose the synthetic fiber and intertwined the colourful threads through her hair, Thando felt overwhelmed at a crossroads. She yearned for guidance and knowledge, which she believed would sharpen her skills and help carve a distinct path in the competitive field. Watching her reflection evolve with each vibrant braid, Thando couldn't keep from pondering the transformation she needed to do within herself to thrive in such a challenging environment.

Thando, feeling stuck and trusting her instincts, decided to reach out to Dennis. She had nowhere else to go. Dennis was the first person who genuinely showed interest in her professional growth. Deep down, she felt certain that if anyone could help her navigate the challenging phase, it would be him. Making an excuse about his workload, Dennis suggested that Thando speak with Hlengiwe, a colleague from Thando's internship days who had risen to a high position within the same department.

Thando wasn't surprised by the recommendation. Hlengiwe, known for her strategic prowess and calm demeanour, was one of the few Black women who had climbed to the top ranks at the company. It felt almost cliché that Dennis would connect her with Hlengiwe, but Thando understood the logic. Who better to guide her than someone who exemplified success and looked like her?

Thando felt disappointed when Hlengiwe mentioned she would be out of the office for the following month.

Undeterred, Thando decided to make the most of her lunch breaks by checking in with her colleagues. She capitalized on the downtimes to get insights from them, sparking conversations about their career journeys, their challenges, and the opportunities they had seized.

Thando delved deeper into her inquiries, and her hopes for her career goals began to waver. Conversations with her senior colleagues, who were primarily Caucasian, emphasized the importance of relentless hard work and dedication, attributing their success to these factors. On the other hand, conversations with members of her community painted a different picture. They highlighted systemic and structural barriers that constrained Black people, limiting their opportunities and success. They spoke of limited training opportunities, persistent discrimination in the workplace, and the difficulty of breaking free from these circumstances against their efforts.

Thando felt frustrated and confused by the conflicting perspectives. The advice from her colleagues and the realities shared by her community muddled her sense of direction. She sensed that the truth might lie between the contrasting worlds, and the realization pushed her to dig deeper. She hoped to uncover the knowledge and insights necessary to navigate the obstacles and find a way forward.

*

Roberta opened her eyes to a different reality and the silent advantages she enjoyed. Roberta's story felt the most real and down-to-earth of all Thando talked to. It was like a lightbulb moment for Thando, bringing her closer to finding the answers she needed. Roberta had started at the company a month before Thando, at the same level, and within six months, she was promoted to Senior Analyst!

Thando's curiosity got the better of her as she leaned in, eager to hear Roberta's secret to success. "How did you move up the ladder so fast?" she asked, intrigued.

Roberta's response was straightforward and unapologetic, illuminating the privileges that had shaped her journey.

"It was the support and guidance from my parents that made all the difference," she explained, pushing a modest tone.

"Both my mom and dad have been my key mentors and motivators. They played a big role in guiding me early in my career, providing valuable insights, and helping me make the right decisions and negotiate my roles. My dad, in particular, has worked in different Executive positions in multinational companies, and his extensive network of contacts has been helpful whenever I needed to connect with different people."

Thando, with poise, tried to mask her impatience as she asked Roberta, "And how did you get the promotion here?"

With a sincere voice, Roberta replied, "Oh, Craig and my dad play golf together, and he recommended me to the director for this position."

When Roberta spoke, Thando felt a tingle of admiration and frustration. She recognized the privilege embedded within Roberta's story—the advantages of having parents who understood the corporate world and had connections & influence to open doors. She did not fault Roberta for her upbringing nor deny her colleague's hard work and talent.

She reflected on her upbringing. While her parents had provided love and support, they didn't have the same skin colour, insider knowledge, or extensive networks as Roberta's parents. The strong contrast in resources and connections deepened Thando's frustration, making her acutely aware of her challenges.

Her upbringing and circumstances were vastly different. She came from a family of farmers and factory workers without mentors or connections in the formal business world. Having family members who could make important introductions or negotiate on her behalf seemed like a distant dream. Financial limitations had shaped her choices thus far, influencing everything from the institution she attended to the duration of her studies. Her parents' expectations were modest, focusing her ambitions on securing a job, even if it meant starting at the bottom rung. Strategic career planning or seeking out influential contacts was far from their reality.

Thando thought of the feedback from her Black colleagues. The stories they shared differed from those of Roberta and her privileged peers. They didn't have family members guiding their every step or making calls on their behalf. The path to success for people like her involved going through social extremes and creating new paradigms. It was a different kind of resilience, born out of necessity and a desire to overcome systemic barriers.

Roberta's question interrupted her train of thought. "Well, didn't you get in here the same way?" she asked, her tone inadvertently coming across as obtuse to Thando. "I see how Craig supports you; I thought he brought you in," she added matter-of-factly.

"Well, it's been quite a journey," Thando replied, her voice tinged with amusement. With a skilful deflection, she steered the conversation away from her struggles. Thando had become adept at navigating her dynamics, skilfully projecting an image of competence and equality.

Admitting that she had stumbled on the job by sheer luck, she felt that without the support of influential connections, she would risk undermining the hard-earned respect she had garnered. She chose to keep her unconventional path a secret, hoping her accomplishments would speak for her in the boardrooms.

*

Thando stared at her phone, her finger hovering over the screen, reading, and rereading the messages in the group chat. The once lively conversations about weddings, babies, and weekend get-togethers had quieted. Her friends had gone down different paths.

The text thread, now filled with chatter, brimmed with pictures of wedding dresses, baby showers, and milestones. Thando slowly scrolled through them, a reminder of how much had changed. The photos of her friends smiling at their bridal parties or cradling newborns felt like windows into a world she couldn't entirely enter. She expressed warmth and congratulations, and each reply felt hollow, unable to express her loneliness.

Thando had devoted herself to her career goals, so the distance between her and her friends grew. She was proud of her professional achievements, and the longing for deep connections lingered, adding another layer to her journey.

She also noticed the difficulties the women on her team faced— the unique struggles and obstacles that seemed to hold them back. They juggled professional responsibilities and family obligations, which put pressure on them to prioritize family matters early on, which slowed down their career advancement. It struck a chord with her, and she deeply empathized with their experiences.

*

Her days had become monotonous, with weekdays bleeding into weekends, leaving Thando increasingly lonely. Long hours, looming deadlines, and demanding projects made it difficult to maintain connections beyond work. The competitive atmosphere at the office didn't help, feeling more adversarial than collaborative. Thando needed a solid support network at work.

Even with the distance between them, Lala provided great comfort. Their meetups in the city were not just occasional; they were bursts of excitement, offering a break from her relentless routine and reminding her of the meaningful connections she still had outside the corporate world.

Lala married her high school sweetheart and embraced the role of a stay-at-home mom, a choice that Thando couldn't fully understand but deeply respected. She observed herself feel a sting of jealousy toward Lala's happiness and fulfillment in her chosen path while grappling with the longing and uncertainty about her aspirations.

While they took different routes in life, their connection remained as strong as ever.

Whenever they had the chance, they would extend invitations to their new friends and rendezvous at lively, bustling restaurants. The clatter of glasses and cheerful chatter added to the mood. These catch-up sessions were like a breath of fresh air, infusing Thando with renewed energy and grounding her in the memories of their carefree student days. Their different paths and life experiences only strengthened their bond of love and friendship, making it unbreakable.

One such evening, a warm summer evening in the streets of downtown Johannesburg. Thando and her friends met at a bustling restaurant with lively chatter and clinking glasses. The place exuded a vibrant and eclectic vibe, with colourful murals adorning the walls and quirky decorations scattered throughout the space. Neon signs flashed catchy slogans, while local artists' artwork in Thembisa added creativity to the atmosphere.

Thando and her friends found their seats, and the restaurant buzzed with energy. Mouthwatering smells wafted from the kitchen, igniting their appetites, and adding to the excitement. Waiters hurried around, serving up plates of delicious food to hungry guests, while upbeat music set the tone for a fun night out.

During one of the many animated conversations among the friends, struggling to hold back, Liza's voice stood out with a pointed question, like a needle piercing through the lively ambiance. "Why do you always focus on the hardships in your life?"

directing her question to Thando, her tone high-pitched and inquisitive.

Liza leaned forward slightly, her expression earnest as she sought to convey her perspective to Thando. Around the table, their friends listened attentively, their faces a mixture of curiosity and empathy.

Thando remained silent, hoping someone else would speak up. It wasn't that she intentionally fixated on her challenges or sought pity from others. Instead, she saw it as a way to release pent-up emotions, to share her raw reality with those she trusted.

With a slight shrug, Liza noticed Thando's discomfort and continued speaking, her words carefully chosen. "Thando, I'm not dismissing your experiences; haven't we all faced tough times?" Her gaze moved around the table, seeking agreement. "Our parents worked hard and sacrificed so we could have opportunities. We can't let those challenges define us," she said gently yet firmly, conveying her belief that Thando was dwelling too much on her difficulties.

There was a moment of silence as Liza's words sank in, the mood in the room shifting slightly. Thando tried to mask her hurt feelings with a forced smile, but the weight of the conversation lingered. "I don't think you guys truly understand what I'm saying. Aren't we all tired of this unfair system?" Her frustration seeped into her voice. "Our parents pour thousands into school fees, hoping it will give us a leg up; it barely makes a difference because the system is rigged." She softened her tone, and her resolve remained firm. "But hey, I get where you're coming from. I'll let it go." Thando realized her friends accepted the status quo and didn't want to burden them further.

Before Thando could finish her sentence, Dudu chimed in. She had a presence that was both calming and insightful. Her warm smile and gentle demeanour often served as a voice of reason during discussions. Her dark, expressive eyes held a deep understanding, reflecting her empathy and wisdom. "Thando, I understand your point, and Liza didn't mean to be harsh. Unfortunately, that's just the way things are. Don't stress yourself out over a system that predominantly favours certain groups. You already have a good job."

Thando kept silent, unsure if Dudu was saying those words to prevent the conversation from escalating or if she truly meant what she said.

Thando managed a forced smile, suppressing her wounded pride, attempting to brush off her defensiveness. She didn't want the disagreement to overshadow the joy of their reunion. Beneath that smile, a flicker of vulnerability remained, an acknowledgment that her friends might never fully understand the intricacies of her experiences.

"I'm sorry if it seems like I'm always talking about my problems," she added, her voice still tinged with defensiveness and accompanied by a hint of vulnerability. I don't mean to dampen our time together. It's just that sharing my challenges helps me process things."

Acknowledging the injustice was an agonizing reality for Thando, one she couldn't easily brush aside. She realized that her friends' coping mechanisms differed from hers, and she grappled with balancing her convictions while maintaining harmony within their unbreakable bond of friendship.

Though undoubtedly truthful, Liza and Dudu's words opened an unhealed wound. Liza pointing out Thando's tendency to complain about her work circumstances struck a chord with Thando —she was carrying guilt and a bag of emotions stemming from the pervasive effects of discrimination. The guilt became a heavy burden for Thando, an invisible weight pressed down on her, clashing with her happy outward appearance. It was a mix of survivor's guilt for leaving behind loved ones still struggling and imposter syndrome, amplified by the nagging doubt of whether she truly deserved to have a seat in the boardroom.

Though unseen by others, the internal struggle weighed heavily on her shoulders, shaping her thoughts and emotions in complex and challenging ways.

*

The next day, Thando sat at her desk in the office, her head heavy from the wine from the dinner meeting that she gushed down her throat, trying to numb the discomfort of the conversation with Liza.

She looked blank, staring at her computer screen, her mind thinking about things outside of work.

II. EMBERS OF AMBITION

Thando imagined a future where she would travel across the continent, leaving a trail of positive impact wherever her footsteps led. She was determined to use her skills and talents to improve her family's life. She looked forward to her career with resolute enthusiasm. She planned her path, working hard to make every dream that lit up her soul come true. Her love for Africa was intensified by her passion. It drove her to overlook her circumstances and focus on her goals.

In the township where Thando grew up, dreams were as common as the sun rising each day. Everyone had something to say about their future aspirations—some shared their dreams eagerly, others recounted failed attempts, while a few whispered about the dreams they believed could still come true. Amidst the sea of aspirations, Thando felt a deep longing. While others focused on their achievements, she yearned to make a tangible difference in her community. Deep down, she understood that her desire to contribute was not just about external impact but also a path to finding inner peace and acceptance.

She leaped to a multinational corporation, hoping to leave stagnation behind and escape Allison. As time passed, her determination transformed into a deep longing and desperation. Comparing her progress to her peers left her disheartened; her career remained stagnant while they advanced, failing to align with her aspirations. Frustration consumed her, tormenting her for not achieving success at the "right" age or in the "ideal" company. Dissatisfied with her job, she tirelessly scoured job listings and networked for new opportunities, yearning for a role that matched her skills and ignited her passion.

Thando's world was changing faster than she could keep up. Instant gratification was the new standard: from 10-day MBA courses to swiping right to find a date, success was just a click away. Thando felt the same pull for immediate victories, just like her peers. Even with her academic achievements, her professional journey was far from smooth.

In meetings, her ideas were dismissed or co-opted by colleagues who took credit. The promotions she had hoped for were given to others despite her qualifications and contributions. Racism and sexism crept into performance reviews, veiled in coded language that cast doubt on her abilities. The systemic bias casts a shadow over her aspirations, making her dreams feel out of reach.

Thando's resolve wavered with each setback, and staying positive became a struggle. Disappointment weighed her down, draining her energy and making it hard to move forward. Success, even when the odds seemed stacked against her.

Phrases such as:

"Everyone should aim to start their own business..."

"Getting a job means becoming a slave to companies..."

"You should hate getting a pay check..."

Made it even more difficult for Thando to stay positive.

Her friends frequently expressed frustration, particularly when discussing how slowly things were changing or lamenting their meagre pay checks. Thando resonated with the dissatisfaction, even in the face of the somewhat negative vibe of the conversations.

She longed for a path to merge her thirst for immediate fulfillment with a deeper purpose. She wanted a way to transcend the ordinary and embrace her brand of success—not merely dictated by societal norms or hasty impulses. The struggle was real, and she knew that her journey toward possible entrepreneurship, or perhaps even the pursuit of her true calling, required a delicate balance between ambition and patience.

Within her community, she witnessed many people trapped in the stagnation of self-reliance. They stubbornly held onto their expertise, unwilling to explore new perspectives or learn from others. Their potential remained untapped, and their aspirations wilted under their pride.

Thando promised herself not to fall victim to her self-imposed confinement. She understood that achieving greatness required courage—a willingness to break free from the comfort of familiarity and seek guidance from those who had already walked the challenging path she aspired to take.

She held a deep-seated belief that traditional employment fostered complacency—a so-called "comfort zone" that stifled growth.

She witnessed firsthand the struggles of individuals who sacrificed their aspirations for financial security. Among them was her close friend, Virginia, a talented painter who had chosen to work in a mundane office job to make ends meet. Thando often admired Virginia's artwork in her small apartment, reminding her of the passion that lay dormant beneath the surface.

It was Percy, her cousin, who touched her nerves. Percy had once dreamed of becoming a renowned musician. His fingers danced effortlessly across the piano keys, captivating everyone who heard him play. The demands of life and the need for a stable income beat and bent down until he abandoned his musical ambitions. He traded his guitar for a desk in the corner of a bustling office. The office's dull fluorescent lighting and the monotonous clicking of keyboards became the soundtrack to his life, a far cry from the melodies he enjoyed creating.

Thando deeply empathized with Virginia and Percy, recognizing the internal conflict they experienced. She knew their pain intimately because she was trapped in a job that brought her no joy or fulfillment. Her exorbitantly high car payments and bond repayments pressed heavily on her shoulders, overshadowing her true passions and aspirations. Not forgetting the pressure she imposed on herself to support her family.

The agony of staying in a detested job slowly chipped away at Thando's spirit. The repetitive tasks and lack of creativity stifled her true potential. Her heart longed to break free from the everyday routine, to follow a path that would set her soul on fire, much like the vibrant paintings of Virginia and the inspiring melodies of Percy. She couldn't ignore the injustices she saw around her, the issues tugged at her conscience. With each passing day, her desire to make a difference grew stronger.

These experiences inspired Thando's perception of business owners, kindling a fire within her soul. They were architects of their destiny to her, forging a path of passion and prosperity.

She observed their focus and felt a magnetic pull toward their world—a world where dreams knew no bounds and limitations were shattered with every breakthrough. She wanted to bask in the radiance of their success, to embrace the intoxicating dance between risk and reward.

In her eyes, their expressed freedom was a testament to their sacrifice and sweat, proof of the resilience and the audacity it took to stand tall amongst a sea of mediocrity.

They were trailblazers, pushing the boundaries of possibility with each calculated leap they took. She wanted the very thing that granted entrepreneurs their perceived freedom.

The captivating vision of immediate achievement enticed her deeply, and she admired the perceived freedom that came with entrepreneurship. However, doubts crept in. *'Could she handle the uncertainty and risk ?'* Her experiences at her corporate job, with its steady structure and defined paths, had shaped her sense of security.

Even knowing it wasn't bringing her the fulfillment she wanted. She was at a crossroads.

The lure of entrepreneurship felt like an exciting yet risky alternative, starkly contrasting the predictable challenges she faced at work. She was vulnerable enough to admit that entrepreneurship wasn't for her then. Her corporate job offered her a playground and platform to learn, allowing her to build skills and experiences she could one day use.

*

In her phase of mental torment, she recalled a conversation she once had with her colleague, Roberta. It sparked an audacious idea that slowly took shape in her troubled mind.

She needed guidance from people ahead of her, though she feared they might mock her ambition. She had experienced that before with Allison, which had backfired. The thought initially felt uncomfortable because Thando had always prided herself on her independence. Deep down, she knew that her dreams would remain out of reach without opening herself up to new perspectives and guidance. She needed to embrace change and step into unfamiliar territory by seeking help beyond her immediate circle.

Gaig and Hlengiwe had not responded, and she knew they were not obligated to help. She was not a victim.

The realization marked a turning point in her thinking. Rather than relying solely on her immediate network, she began to open her mind to exploring new avenues of connecting with people who could expand her perspective.

Braids In The Boardroom

Hey, black child.
Do you know where you are going?
Where you're going
Do you know you can learn?
What you want to learn
What you can learn

*

Thando's once vibrant social life had dimmed to a mere flicker, overshadowed by the demands of her stagnant career. She watched her friends move on with their lives and felt a growing sense of disconnection. Each day, the corporate world widened the gap between her and those she once shared dreams with. The unfamiliar territory of boardroom politics and office hierarchies only added to her sense of isolation. In the tumult, Thando longed for clarity to guide her through the murky waters of uncertainty, to light a path toward a future that felt truly hers.

In the quiet hum of the office, Thando noticed how her colleagues sneakily monitored each other's social media activities. She observed the casual glances at screens turn into whispered discussions and influence office decisions.

It troubled her deeply. While she understood that people had lives outside of work, she felt uneasy witnessing personal matters being used as grounds for professional judgments.

One particular incident stuck with her. A colleague's promotion was derailed due to a seemingly harmless social media post; she was seen to be "flashy and not needing" a big head.

Thando couldn't shake off the injustice of it all. Yet her discomfort, she chose silence. She recognized the potential repercussions of speaking up. So, she consciously decided to keep her personal life private at work. She tightened her privacy settings and blocked her coworkers from accessing her social media activities, determined to safeguard her boundaries in the face of office scrutiny

*

Days turned into weeks, and Thando's quest for clarity only deepened. She found herself drawn to the stories of her family's past, hoping to uncover clues that might make sense of her path.

No amount of reading or relaxation could quiet Thando's restless mind. She looked for comfort, hoping to find a sense of belonging. She joined networking events and social clubs, eager to connect with others navigating similar paths.

Nothing could ease her soul; with every interaction, she grappled with more questions than answers.

Feeling a deep pull, Thando resolved to travel to her grandmother's home in the heart of KwaDukuza, fondly referred to as 'The Original Home' by her and her cousins. The name 'KwaDukuza' translates to 'Place of the Lost Person' in Zulu, although its true meaning runs deeper than its literal translation. While the modern world moved forward with its impersonal developments and towering skyscrapers, the humble village remained true to its soul. It was like a tapestry of emerald fields and modest mud dwellings that whispered stories of a simpler time, where tradition and community seamlessly intertwined.

Thando cruised in her sleek electric blue BMW X1 along the freshly laid roads that linked her village founded by King Shaka to the broader world. Notwithstanding the premium instalments she diligently paid, the car was more than just a mode of transportation—it symbolized her hard work and determination to succeed. She journeyed through the scenic route and felt a profound connection to her roots. The rolling hills and majestic mountains enveloped her, providing solace and a sense of belonging. The symphony of nature, with its rustling leaves and chirping birds, made her senses come alive. Thando embraced the beauty of the unspoiled surroundings in that tranquil moment, cherishing each unfolding moment.

Opening her car window, Thando welcomed the refreshing breeze that tousled her long braids, filling her lungs with the invigorating scent of fertile soil and the promise of new beginnings. The sun, shining brightly in the sky, painted the path before her in a radiant golden light, enveloping the serene meadows in a warm and comforting embrace. Sheep and cattle peacefully grazed on the lush greenery, adding to the idyllic beauty of the scene. In the distance, a modest kraal symbolized the enduring relationship between the villagers and the land that sustained them. Nearby, a thriving maize garden whispered tales of abundance and nourishment.

Thando carefully maneuvered her car along the twisting dirt road; the tires stirred up a vibrant cloud of red dust, adding a touch of wildness to her journey. Each particle of dust carried the essence of the vibrant land, creating an almost magical aura that swirled around her car as if the very earth rejoiced in her return, offering a long-awaited embrace.

She approached her family's ancestral kraal Homestead, and happiness bubbled up inside her. The Homestead, tucked away in the heart of KwaDukuza, held a special place in her heart. Her cousins, who still lived there, were cattle farmers, each with a cozy mud house within the compound.

Taking in the scene, Thando admired the lush maize food garden to the right of the kraal and watched as chickens roamed freely around the yard, adding to the rustic charm of the scene.

Opening the creaking wooden fence, Thando felt a rush of nostalgia. Crafted with love by her cousins, the fence whispered secrets of generations past, a tangible reminder of the family's deep connection to the land.

*

Thando walked in and immediately spotted her grandmother seated on the floor, surrounded by other women from the community, all gathered on an African Zulu Woven Embroidered Mat called icansi. Nestled within the circle of wise women, her grandmother exuded an aura of quiet authority that effortlessly commanded attention.

Watching them interact, Thando marvelled at the ease with which they laughed and shared stories. Their voices carried the weight of wisdom and experience, weaving a tapestry of shared knowledge and history.

As soon as she set eyes on her grandmother. Thando felt a rush of warmth engulf her heart. An unspoken language of love passed between them, connecting their souls. Her grandmother's eyes twinkled with pride, the wrinkles on her face telling stories of a life well-lived.

Thando joined the circle of women on the icons without even pausing to consider unpacking the car. They didn't hesitate to make room for her, welcoming her as if they had eagerly awaited her arrival. At that moment, nothing else mattered to her but the profound sense of belonging she felt among them.

When she settled in, her grandmother pulled her close, enveloping her in a warm embrace that spoke volumes of their bond. In their presence, Thando shared an extraordinary connection with her Gogo. While her parents played their part in shaping her life, her grandmother added vibrant hues to her world. Together, they had painted beautiful memories, exchanging secrets, dreams, and laughter that bound them together forever.

*

Late nights in their cozy four-room house felt like a sanctuary. Time slowed down, and joy was all around. They entertained gossip about quirky neighbours and mischievous relatives in the thick of the warmth of Gogo's laughter. Unpacking the complexity of their lively community with humour.

In their playful exchanges, Gogo had a special way of transporting Thando back in time with her captivating stories. With a sparkle in her eyes and a gentle grin, she would weave tales of her youth. Painting vivid pictures of how she first met Thando's late grandfather—a tale brimming with romance and nostalgia. These precious moments weren't just stories. They were windows into Thando's family history, reminders of the timeless strength of love that bound them together.

Thando cherished every moment spent with her Gogo, eagerly soaking up the tales of a bygone era. Her grandmother reminisced about the "good old days," her face brightened with joy.

What if Gogo had been able to chase her dreams wholeheartedly, unrestricted by the former oppressive government and societal norms 'Thando pondered.' Who would she be to me and the world ?"

Thando imagined a world where Gogo's untapped potential had flourished, in awe of her grandmother's resilience.

Thando often marvelled at her grandmother's resilience. Though she faced oppression during apartheid, her Gogo served as a nurse, caring for those who were also responsible for her suffering. After retirement, she used her experience and skills to serve as a community nurse. Gogo's unwavering dedication to easing the suffering of others, even in the face of adversity, deeply moved Thando.

Gogo shared her stories with a thankful heart, discussing the times she had to sacrifice and work hard. Even though she didn't get much in return, she was grateful for what she had. Listening to her, Thando began viewing her life through a new lens, contemplating how to make the best of what she had. Thando would be thoroughly entertained by Gogo's stories of her younger days, especially the ones involving her romantic escapades. Gogo's lively tales had Thando hooked, imagining everything as if she were watching a captivating rom-com play out in real life. The image of a young Gogo charming her admirers with her wit and charisma painted a funny yet heartwarming scene. Thando giggled along with Gogo, relishing every moment of the amusing and relatable stories from her grandmother's past.

Gogo shared one of the most entertaining stories about how she chose Thando's grandfather over a neighbour boy who later joined the freedom movement. Gogo recounted how she was pursued by both suitors, but ultimately, her heart belonged to Thando's grandfather. She described the comical antics of the neighbour boy as he tried to win her affection, from bringing her flowers to attempting to serenade her under the moonlight. Despite his efforts, Gogo remained steadfast in her decision to be with Thando's grandfather.

Even though Gogo missed her beloved husband, she embraced her independence as a woman in her seventies. With every passing day, she revelled in the freedom to explore life's limitless possibilities. Thando admired her grandmother's resilience and determination to live life on her terms, even after losing her partner.

*

From an early age, Thando recognized that Gogo was no ordinary woman. It wasn't just the unique way her grandmother decorated their house but also the subtle rebellion she embodied. While other grandmothers in their neighbourhood proudly displayed religious portraits of Jesus in their living rooms, Gogo chose to defy societal norms by showcasing a striking image of Shaka Zulu, portrayed by the legendary Henry Cele, in his traditional attire.

The unconventional choice was more than just an aesthetic statement; it symbolized Gogo's defiance against the unspoken rules governing their community. Gogo refused to conform, daring to challenge the expectations imposed upon her by tradition and culture.

"Don't get married," Gogo often proclaimed, her words etching deeply into Thando's impressionable mind. But her message went beyond mere avoidance of matrimony; it was a call to Thando to live life on her terms. Gogo's advice to her granddaughter carried a subtle hint of sarcasm as if suggesting wisdom from another world,

"Have fun, fall in love, enjoy life with whomever you choose as your partner. And whatever you do, don't get married."

Gogo understood that in their culture, marriage often meant suppressing one's desires and dreams in favour of fulfilling the needs of a husband. She refused to subject any of her grandkids, especially Thando, to such a fate. Gogo was determined to shield them from the constraints of societal expectations and allow them to pursue their dreams without compromise.

Only when she was older did Thando understand the profound wisdom behind Gogo's unconventional beliefs. Her grandmother's rebellious spirit had seeped into her veins, instilling the courage to challenge the status quo and forge her path. Gogo's unconventional I was not just an expression of personal taste but a powerful symbol of resistance against the oppressive norms that stifled her individuality and freedom.

*

In the embrace of her grandmother's love, Thando was free to share her deepest hopes and aspirations. Their bond was a haven where dreams could flourish and reach their grandest heights without judgment. With each conversation, Thando eagerly unveiled her desire to join the ranks of those who seized every opportunity life offered. She spoke of the C-Suite executives who sat in board-rooms, dictating the price of bread, the number of jobs to be created, and the infrastructure improvements needed to uplift communities. Perhaps one day, she could influence decisions to improve her community. She yearned to explore the world, venturing into lands unjustly denied to her people. Speaking with her Gogo, Thando expressed her longing to study in foreign countries, breaking free from the suffocating stereotypes that clung to young black girls like heavy shackles.

Gogo, always a beacon of loving support, listened intently to Thando's words, her eyes brimming with excitement. She relished seeing the world through Thando's eyes. In her responses, she offered assurance that these dreams were within immediate reach. Her confidence and hope mirrored the sentiments of Mr. Perkins' empowering poem,

> "Hey Black Child, do you know you can be what you want to be?"

During their precious moments together, her grandmother would remind her of the importance of holding on to her faith. Thando absorbed these teachings with a deep understanding of their value growing up. Like her cousins, she drifted away from the core of her grandmother's wisdom as she went about her life. The discord of her struggles and obstacles reverberated within her mind, causing doubt to seep into the beliefs she was raised to hold dear.

On her visits, Gogo reminded Thando of the significance of nurturing a relationship with God, a tradition they honoured by attending the modest neighbourhood church. The old church stood as a timeless testament to faith and devotion. Its weathered stone walls were covered with marks of countless seasons, each crack and crevice whispering stories of generations past.

When Thando and Gogo entered its hallowed doors, the church had a simple and cozy charm. They were greeted by the scent of aged wooden pews and the soft glow of stained-glass windows that filtered the sunlight into a kaleidoscope of colours. The fragrance inside carried peace and tranquillity, inviting visitors to leave their worries at the threshold and sink themselves into the embrace of something greater.

The group of people in the church was small, about twenty, and they were very close, like a big family. Each person had their own story, filled with laughter and tears. They gathered weekly to share their joys and troubles, finding support in their faith. It was a friendly place where everyone knew each other's names and welcomed newcomers.

On that particular visit, Gogo stood at the front with a unique presence that felt spiritual and wise. Her voice, aged by years of devotion, had an authority that seemed to come from another time. She recited a cherished verse from Proverbs 19:18, "Where there is no vision, the people perish," and it felt like her words filled the whole church, reminding everyone about the importance of having hope and purpose.

Gogo prayed for Thando with heartfelt intensity, and it was as though the sacred space embraced them both, guiding them with a gentle touch.

'God must BE a Woman!' Thando mused, absorbing the electrifying atmosphere of the church. It was like divine energy was moving in the pews, a tangible unity and devotion that lifted them together. Their hearts were entwined in a shared reverence.

*

On one of the days, Thando's grandmother received an unexpected visitor from the neighbouring village, Mam'Jezi.

Such unannounced visits were common, given the vast distances between the villages, which often ranged from 15 to 30 kilometres. Sometimes, the journey required navigating rough terrain and crossing rivers, which was only possible during low tides, adding further time to the travel.

In the tight-knit community, visitors were regarded as auspicious and warmly embraced for the considerable effort it took to cross the challenging terrain.

Mam'Jezi, a charismatic social butterfly, held a special place in the village. She was known for her outgoing nature and knack for effortlessly delving into everyone's lives, including her family. People often tried to maintain a tight-lipped demeanour around her, but her captivating and inquisitive way of posing questions had a way of loosening tongues within seconds.

Gogo did not call her a gossiper; instead, she described her as someone known for oversharing information about people's lives. Such was Gogo's character, always finding a gentle way to address controversial topics.

"Wow, city girl," Mam'Jezi trilled with delight. "My ancestors told me something surprising was waiting for me here." Her excitement was palpable as she stepped inside, making herself comfortable on Gogo's favourite spot on Gogo's corner couch.

She emphasized her urgent need for a refreshing drink with an urgent, pointed gesture toward the refrigerator.

"Woza la, Mtwanami," she beckoned Thando, enveloping her warmly.

"Come and enlighten me about your city life adventures."

Gogo interrupted their embrace, shaking her head with laughter. "Mam'Jezi, you've come from afar. Spare the children, and let's chat," she reminded Mam'Jezi that her visit was intended for the elders' company rather than entertaining the youngsters.

"On my way here, I passed by Mam'Nkosi's house for a night. Let me tell you, it was a night that seemed to stretch on forever," Mam'Jezi shared, a tinge of sarcasm lacing her words.

She emphasized her discomfort by holding her waist as if to physically convey the agony of the bed.

Switching topics quickly to avoid Gogo's correction ."Do you remember that lanky son of hers, the firstborn?" She snapped her fingers, attempting to jog her memory with closed eyes.

„U Jabu or U NkosiUnamandla?" Gogo asked, well-acquainted with the children.

"Yebo, MuziUnaMandla!" Mam'Jezi confirmed, her expression reflecting her bewilderment at the choice of such names. "I mean, who in their right mind would punish their kids with such names," she shrugged. Thando couldn't contain her laughter, finding Mam'Jezi's reactions utterly amusing.

"You did an excellent job naming your children with such lovely names, just like this one, Thando," Mam'Jezi attempted to flatter Gogo, hoping to gain an active role in their conversations.

Gogo chuckled heartily, aware of Mam'Jezi's tactics.

"And what about that sweet boy?" she inquired, eagerly awaiting the gossip.

"I've heard he's become quite the big shot in the city after securing a lucrative contract with one of those influential government figures," Mam'Jezi announced, applauding with mock enthusiasm.

"He even renovated Mam'Nkosi's house, adding a self-flushing toilet in her bedroom!" She was amused

"Now she doesn't need to wipe herself; talk about luxurious living! "She giggled.

"That's wonderful," Gogo exclaimed, genuinely pleased. I would also be happy if I didn't need to bother with that sandpaper of toilet paper.

"Yes, his mother mentioned that he's now mentoring young men in the village, teaching them the ways of business," Mam'Jezi continued, pausing for effect.

"He's positively impacting the young boys in the village as well."

"Mam 'Nkosi truly did an outstanding job raising those children on her own, considering what she went through," Gogo commented, sighing.

When she spoke, her eyes gleamed with the memories of a powerful black woman.

"I remember how her husband's violent outbursts plagued their lives, haunting their every moment. She endured countless nights of fear, and he finally left her for dead."

That day was the hardest for the community. "Uyakhumbula Mam'Jezi expected Mam'Jezi to remember the story as she was thinking. Gogo and her friends had a remarkable way of communicating. Their words flowed seamlessly, interweaving and completing each other's sentences as if they shared a telepathic bond. It was as if they possessed an uncanny ability to anticipate each other's thoughts and effortlessly delve into the intricate details of their lives. Witnessing their camaraderie was like observing a beautifully choreographed dance of connection and understanding.

"That day is etched in my mind when that savage of a man's rage reached its pinnacle. He unleashed a brutal assault on Mam 'Nkosi, thinking he had succeeded in ending her life. God had different plans for her and her children.! "She said with a mingle of relief and gratitude, holding back tears of joy.

"I still can't believe he left her and went drinking with prostitutes at the tavern," Mam'Jezi added. "With her husband gone,

Mam 'Nkosi rose from the ashes of her pain. She fought tirelessly, working odd jobs to make ends meet. While facing the challenges, she still tried selling peanuts at nearby schools. It was her humble means to provide for her children's education." She added that she was looking at Thando to emphasize that they recounted the story for her.

Ultimately, all of Mam'Nkosi's hard work paid off. Armed with the wisdom and strength they inherited from their mother, her children went out into the world with determination.

Gogo's voice wavered as she finished, saying, "It shows how strong she was and what can happen when love and determination come together. Mam'Nkosi's story should be shared and honoured." Thank goodness they had two brain cells to rub together, unlike their loser of a father. " Mam'Jezi could not help herself together, her notorious character showing its head.

"Oh, Mam'Jezi!" Gogo exclaimed, her laughter bursting. She covered her face with her gently wrinkled hands. I was wondering when that side of you would show its head," and they all burst out in laughter.

*

Thando's heart skipped. Mam'Jezi's words echoed in her mind. The idea of a mentor and a sponsor struck a chord, taking it as a clear sign she needed guidance.

' *How could I have missed the idea of looking for a mentor or a sponsor?'* A realization rested on her, shedding light on the path she had been wandering.

Mam'Jezi's words confirmed that a mentor could help her get clear on the next steps in her career. The idea resonated with her. It conjured images of fresh perspectives.

It called on her for the courage to challenge norms. And the promise of gaining invaluable wisdom to expand her horizons.

III. RISING TO RECOGNITION

Thando's mother stood as a beacon of unflinching strength in the vast continent, where resilience ran deep. Thando grew up observing her mother's relentless efforts in every aspect of life, even in her unfulfilling marriage to her father. Her mother's strong work ethic left an indelible impression on Thando. Her mother seldom paused to assess the outcomes of their endeavors. For her, progress took a backseat to their firm commitment and the belief that her hard work would one day be recognized and rewarded, perhaps even by God.

Inspired by her mother's relentless work ethic, Thando brought the same strong determination to her job. Every day, she was the first to walk into the office at eight in the morning and the last to leave at seven in the evening. Her commitment didn't stop there; Thando always signed up for extra courses to boost her skills and jumped at the chance to take on the challenging projects everyone else steered clear of.

These weren't just actions to get ahead; they were a nod to her mother's lasting impact on her approach to work. Thando's commitment to doing her best shone through in the quality of her work, which consistently went above and beyond what was expected.

She valued her time, not wanting to miss a beat, and she made it a point to be punctual for every meeting, never leaving others waiting. Late into the evenings, when her manager sent group emails and WhatsApp texts, Thando was the first to respond, trying to prove her tenacious dedication to the team's success. She was convinced that her willingness to go the extra mile was valued by everyone around her.

*

The day of her performance review came, and she was excited to get the positive affirmations she craved. She had poured her heart and soul into her work, going above and beyond to exceed expectations. Finally, it seemed like her efforts would be acknowledged.

Her boss greeted her with a warm smile and wasted no time expressing his appreciation for her exceptional performance. Thando felt a surge of pride, knowing that her hard work had not gone unnoticed.

"In recognition of your outstanding contributions, Thando, we have decided to give you a well-deserved 40% salary increase, way above the average industry standard," her lie manager announced, his voice laced with enthusiasm. Thando's heart swelled with joy when

she absorbed the news. It was a tangible validation of her dedication and talent.

Instead, the excitement was short-lived as her line manager continued. "And now, I have an important announcement. Our team's performance has been exceptional over the past two years, largely thanks to your invaluable contributions. As a result, we have been given additional resources to handle the increased workload."

Thando's excitement waned when the conversation was not playing out according to her script.

"To ensure efficient management of this expanded team, we have appointed Frans Du Plessis as the new Head of Finance." Thando's jaw dropped, her mind struggling to process the news. France was the last person she expected to be chosen for such a role.

"France Du Plessis?" she blurted out, her voice not hiding her disbelief. The mere thought of Frans overseeing the finance department was inconceivable to her. Thando had known Frans for a while and had described him to her friends as someone with an arrogant and lazy personality.

Her line manager nodded, seemingly oblivious to the emotional turmoil brewing within Thando. "Yes, France has demonstrated exceptional leadership potential, and we believe he is the right person to guide the team in this new phase. We trust that you will work well together under his guidance."

All kinds of thoughts raced through Thando's mind, a hurricane of confusion and frustration. Thando struggled to find her voice in the sea of emotions crashing within her. She couldn't fathom how France, who carried a chip of superiority on his shoulders, strutted around the office, rarely engaging in meaningful conversations with his colleagues and often dismissing their ideas without giving them a second, was the one who got prompted.

His arrogance extended to his work ethic—or rather, the lack of it. Frans had a reputation for procrastination and frequently passing off his responsibilities to others. He had no qualms about shirking his duties, expecting others to pick up the slack while he coasted through the workday with minimal effort. Thando had often seen him reclining back in his chair, his beloved Veldskoen shoes propped up on his desk, seemingly more interested in browsing the internet for non-work-related content than fulfilling his job obligations.

Her line manager continued to justify the decision, and Thando's anger and disappointment grew. She had dedicated countless hours to extra unpaid projects, sacrificing her time for the team's betterment. Ultimately, her efforts seemed futile, and her hard work was seemingly overlooked, but she was rewarded with more work.

The very sight of France after that meeting- by no fault of his own, only intensified her seething anger. Frustrated and desperate for an escape, she left the office early and met up with a friend to vent her frustrations.

*

She briskly walked inside the I. Her friend Ray, who had an uncanny talent for creating humor out of the most obscure situations, caught sight of Thando and waved his hands with gestures of urgency, motioning for her to join him at a secluded table across the dimly lit bar. Beyond his humor, Ray was incredibly supportive and caring.

They last saw each other a month before, when he married his long-term boyfriend, Jake. He still radiated an upbeat and joyful spirit infectious to those around him. A glass of Chardonnay awaited her on the table, accompanied by a warm smile that instantly put her at ease. As perceptive as ever, Ray sensed the urgency in her request to meet and knew she was grappling with a challenging day.

"You read my mind," she said, grateful for Ray's intuitive understanding. Thando took the drink in her hand, relishing its coolness, and reached for the chair, eager to sink into its comfort.

Time flew as they lost themselves in a deep and genuine conversation, neither noticing the hour slipping away. Thando's furrowed brow and tight-lipped silence conveyed her frustration, while Ray's nods and thoughtful pauses showed his understanding of her reservations.

"Sometimes, working hard can seem pointless if it doesn't yield the desired results. Look around you, and you'll see people who give everything they have to their work but aren't recognized for it. They often miss the subtle signs in the office environment." Supporting her sentiment of not being recognized.

Seeing Thando's predicament and how hard she had worked to get to the next level in her career, he empathetically offered a solution. He proposed introducing her to his Human Resource manager, who was also his close friend.

Thando felt that even though she had been progressing in her career, she could learn a lot about corporate advancement.

"That's exactly what I need," Thando exclaimed, her voice dripping with sarcasm, picking up from Ray's humorous comments. I need Someone who approves these obscure promotions to enlighten me on how on earth mediocre people manage to rise the ranks."

Her remark elicited a burst of raucous laughter that caught the bartender's attention. He glanced across the table, intrigued by the unexpected roar of laughter.

He chuckled, shaking his head in amusement. "Damn, this working world is one crazy-ass ride," he added. "Sounds like you work at a talent show, and these promotions must be the crème de la crème of undercover karaoke battles."

"Oh, it's just the comedy of corporate life," Thando entertained the banter.

*

When Thando met the H.R. manager Ray recommended, she regained her calm about the situation. Though she had overcome her emotional state, she could not attend work without feeling disappointed.

When Thando arrived at his office, Ray gave her a big hug. Together, they walked up to the second floor of the H.R. manager's office. Acting like he was showing an old friend around, Ray ushered Thando inside with a playful grin and then peeked back through the door, giving her a wink to signal that they were on schedule.

"Welcome," greeted the H.R. manager with a polite and distinctly heavy Afrikaans accent. The light in the room highlighted her long, fiery red hair. She took confident strides towards Thando, seemingly unfazed by her oversized dress that was mopping the floor. She opened her arms wide with a warm smile as if welcoming a long-lost daughter. At that moment, Thando surrendered to the comforting embrace, cherishing the scent of her dominant rose fragrance. It was exactly what she needed – a tender and warm gesture that eased her troubled mind.

Karryn Murray, the Director of Human Resources, introduced herself with a unique twist. "It's Karryn with a 'K,' not a 'C,'" she pointed out, emphasizing the uncommon spelling of her name. She quickly explained that meeting with outsiders wasn't typical for her, but she made an exception for Thando as a favor to her friend, Ray.

Thando eased into a plush chair by the elegant mahogany desk, the softness enveloping her. She accepted a glass of cold water, took a refreshing sip, and exhaled deeply, feeling the tension melt away as she settled in for the conversation.

Karryn inquired, her Afrikaans accent adding a touch of charm to her words, "Ray told me that you recently had a disappointing promotion discussion with your manager. Am I correct?" She searched for the right words, navigating her limited English vocabulary.

Listening intently without interruption, she got up from her chair. She strolled towards her office window, which gave her a view of the beautiful office park adorned with graceful antelopes and majestic peacocks wandering the gardens. Keeping her back to Thando, she kept nodding, showing she was completely focused and genuinely interested in her story.

"Well," she replied, "There isn't just one solution to the challenge, but based on my more than twenty years of experience in this field, I can tell you that three factors have had a significant impact on why you haven't received the promotion, or rather, why some people do get promoted."

She continued and gestured with her right index finger to emphasize her points. Thando took out her notebook and started making notes:

"Your ability to position yourself".

"Early in my career, I found myself frustrated and looking for guidance on advancing into a more senior role within my company. Unnoticed and still treated as a junior even after having the necessary qualifications, I reached out to a mentor for advice. In our conversation, he shared a sentence that profoundly impacted me: "Positioning is 90% acquisition." Initially confused, I asked him to elaborate.

He explained "that to be considered for the position I wanted, I needed to act and behave as if I already held that role. It wasn't enough to wait for an appointment; I had to proactively communicate that I was ready for the next level and demonstrate that I had gained the skills and capabilities necessary to perform the job. Inspired by the advice, I acted, and viola!" she opened her hand like she was about to break into a dance.

I approached a colleague currently in the role I aspired to and asked if I could shadow him once a week. That allowed me to learn firsthand about the job responsibilities and the associated terminology. I also seized the opportunity to attend customer meetings with him and offered to assist with reports and presentations. My colleague was delighted to have an eager assistant, and my manager at the time supported the initiative.

"You must blow your own horn".

Karryn explained that many employees miss out on promotions or opportunities for advancement because senior managers and decision-makers are unaware of their contributions or their existence within the organization. Instead, they often rely on their immediate managers to advocate for them during promotion discussions. If Thando could present concrete evidence of her accomplishments, she would demonstrate that she wasn't looking for an increase or promotion without doing the necessary work.

"Don't be shy to talk about yourself at work," Karryn encouraged, her accent getting heavier as she spoke. Thando, momentarily distracted by it, snapped back to attention. "It's not bragging," she added firmly.

"I know women are less willing to promote themselves," Karryn continued, with the same earnest tone, "but hey, it's all part of the game. Besides, who else will blow your horn if not you?" She gave Thando a knowing look, her lips curling into a playful smile

Thando felt a pang of unease at Karryn's words, her upbringing flashing through her mind. At home, humility and modesty had been cherished, with self-promotion viewed as self-centered. Her hands instinctively sweating at the behavior Karryn was suggesting.

But Thando knew she had to adapt. She took a deep breath, her stomach in knots at the thought of shifting from the familiar path of humility to a more self assertive approach.

Karryn continued, explaining the importance of positioning oneself within the company. She stressed the importance of understanding the internal dynamics and their intersecting with the external environment. Thando needed to observe decision-making processes, identify key decision-makers and influencers, and understand how changes were implemented.

Karryn emphasized more than Thando could count. She needed to grasp how it operated to thrive in the corporate environment. She shared how she advised newcomers, particularly interns, to spend their initial two to three months in an organization as a learning and observation period while also fulfilling their job responsibilities. The phase required active listening and limited speaking. Once Thando understood how the organization functioned, she could initiate follow-up meetings with key stakeholders and engage with influential individuals in her desired area of expertise. Armed with a better understanding of the company's workings, she could confidently share her ideas, suggestions, and opinions with the relevant people, propelling the business forward.

Her last point got Thando's attention.

"The squeakiest wheel gets the most attention, and the harder you work, the more work you get. "Karyn looked at Thando, knowing she had just confused her paradigm.

" Listen to me clearly. Working smart gets you positive rewards, and working hard gets you more work, " Karyn continued, her index finger still instructing.

Karryn could see Thando's perplexed look, but it all made sense; she could see it in her situation. The harder she worked, the more work she was given.

"So how do I work hard and get results then? " Thando asks, shrugging her shoulders.

"AHA! Now you are asking the right question. " Karryn smiled.

"You work smart, my dear. You finish each project, and you do what I told you. You blow your horn about the effort it took and the results!" she said, clenching her fist to show determination.

"You celebrate the end of one project before rushing to the next. " Karyn paused to make sure Thando was paying attention.

"Oh, and don't quote me on the last point, " letting out a naughty laugh while walking her out of their office.

*

In just two years, Thando's workplace had drastically changed due to economic pressures and frequent management reshuffles. Everything that once seemed stable was uncertain.

The company's decision to revamp its reporting structures led to a harsh round of layoffs. The office environment, previously a hub of friendship and collaboration, was tainted with conversations of fear, sadness, and uncertainty. The layoffs left those who remained feeling betrayed and insecure, deeply shaking the sense of community that had once been a cornerstone of the workplace.

Adding to the turmoil, the company closed offices in crucial markets, causing further disarray among employees and clients. Everyone was left scrambling to understand the extent of these changes and worrying about their future with the company.

Old routines and structures that had been the norm for years were suddenly abandoned, making the office feel alien. Everyone started reminiscing on the " good old days." The shift to outsourced services introduced new challenges, complicating a difficult situation. Employees had to quickly adapt to new procedures and roles, grappling with the changes while still dealing with the fallout from the layoffs.

Every day brought a fresh storm of change at Thando's workplace, challenging her to navigate a landscape of relentless uncertainty. Standing firm, she drew strength from the unity among her colleagues. As layoff announcements echoed through the halls, the office climate filled with the somber sounds of farewells among long-time friends. In these moments, Thando and her colleagues wove a tight-knit web of support, their shared resilience transforming the workplace into a bastion of solidarity.

The period was a crucible of both daunting challenges and hidden growth opportunities. Despite the swirling uncertainty, Thando clung to a thread of hope for the organization's recovery.

The emotional toll of the layoffs spilled over onto social media, where many employees shared their raw feelings and personal stories. The virtual space brimmed with poignant posts while hashtags like #CompanyChanges, #LayoffReality, and #UncertainTimes trended, drawing together a community of voices searching for comfort and camaraderie. While these decisions were strategically sound, they cast a shadow over the company's spirit, clouding the judgment of even the senior management.

When management proposed a two-day offsite team-building event, Thando saw it as a perfect chance to shake off the office gloom and connect with her colleagues. She was excited about the opportunity to strengthen team bonds, improve collaboration, and build a more united team spirit. Thando was eager to participate in fun, engaging activities, looking forward to a break that promised to bring a wave of positive energy.

*

Excitement buzzed in the office, and all those left behind after the layoffs eagerly boarded the bus to take them to an offsite resort for a much-anticipated team-building event. The bus rolled forward, and Thando sat by the window, watching her colleagues' superficial and strained interactions unfold.

It became painfully obvious that the usual office hierarchy and departmental boundaries had followed them onto the bus. People from different levels of authority and departments didn't seem to interact much, sticking to their familiar circles. The atmosphere was not gloomy, but there was an underlying sense that many viewed the offsite as more of a necessary obligation than a chance for genuine bonding.

Thando noticed that those in higher positions within the company were engaged in lively conversations, effortlessly chatting away, while the junior staff appeared more reserved and quieter. Some stared out the window with earphones plugged into their ears, perhaps seeking solace in their music within the unfamiliarity.

The scene reminded Thando of high school drama, where cliques and social hierarchies were established. It was as if the "cool kids" had claimed their positions at the front of the bus, confident and boisterous, while others seemed to fade into the background.

The conference attendees arrived, and the management teams from different departments agreed to meet for a meeting before dinner to set the tone before the event. They had reserved a boardroom in one of the conference rooms, which offered a beautiful view of the field where the team-building activities would occur. It was the beginning of spring, with flowers blooming and a gentle breeze carrying the last traces of winter. The scene was picturesque, creating the perfect atmosphere for discussions.

Greg Horn, the region's vice president, initiated the management meeting, setting a relaxed and welcoming tone. He was casually dressed in khaki shorts, a Caucasian baseball cap, a blue golf shirt, and clean, brand-new Caucasian running shoes. He sat at the head of a round table, with a blank chart paper beside him.

The team members took their seats, the room full of anticipation. Thando walked into the meeting room, her gaze sweeping over the familiar sight of notepads and coffee mugs prepared for the discussion. She settled into her chair, and a quiet realization came to her—she was the only black woman in the room. It wasn't a new experience for her; there had been many such rooms. Initially, these moments had made her think she was unique, almost celebrated, as if she were breaking new ground. But as time passed, that initial pride faded into a more somber reflection. Each such instance became a reminder of the isolation and the slow pace of change in diversity.

The excitement of being "unique" had worn off. Thando became more aware of the biases that still existed in society. Being the only black person in the room reminded her of the unfair prejudices that some people held to. It hurt to know that she had to face subtle racism just to thrive in such a place.

Thando was tired of dealing with the ignorance. It wasn't glamorous to succeed in a society that didn't fully understand or appreciate her experiences as a black woman. The idea of being exclusive lost its appeal when she realized it came with enduring hurtful comments and biases.

Being the only black person in the room wasn't something she enjoyed. She didn't want to constantly prove herself and her worth just because of her skin color. Thando dreamed of a world where her achievements and skills would be recognized for what they truly were without being overshadowed by her appearance.

The first Item on the agenda was Arnold, the operations team manager. He provided an update on his department's progress and outlined the desired outcomes for the upcoming team-building activity. These objectives resonated with everyone: boosting team morale, increasing revenue, and effectively allocating resources for success.

After Arnold finished his update, the team unanimously agreed that sharing these objectives with their respective teams was important. Still, Thando believed that cross-collaboration between teams was another aspect that needed attention. She suggested implementing a standardized template for sharing progress updates on collaborative projects. That would ensure transparency and facilitate effective communication. Recognizing the value of Thando's suggestion, Greg expressed his support.

But then, the peaceful atmosphere was shattered by an unexpected interruption from the back of the room. Frans, a team member, raised his voice accusingly, questioning Thando's demeanor. With his pen still in hand, he exclaimed, "Why are you always angry? Why must you challenge, add to, or disagree with everything?" His words were loud, disrupting the previously harmonious environment.

Taken aback by the sudden confrontation, Thando managed to maintain her composure. Acting swiftly to diffuse the tension, Greg intervened and redirected his attention to Frans. "Frans, could you please elaborate on what specifically about Thando's point seemed angry ?"

The room fell into stunned silence, and the rest of the team looked shocked at his words, waiting for Frans's response.

Frans shrugged nonchalantly, his words hanging like a heavy cloud. The room descended into a stunned silence, with the rest of the team looking visibly shocked by his unexpected admission.

Frans's promotion over Thando had sparked a simmering conflict between them. Frans, eager to assert his newfound authority and seniority, did not miss an opportunity. Sensing the mounting tension, Greg intervened, aiming to mediate the situation.

"So, to clarify," he said, his voice unable to mask the surprise and concern. "Do you agree with Thando's suggestion to add the reviews?"

Thando's mind raced, emotions swirling within her. At that moment, she felt a surge of disbelief and frustration. "WOW," she exclaimed, her voice blending astonishment and hurt. She settled back into her chair, wearing dark blue jeans and a crisp, pristine white shirt. With a deliberate gesture, she rolled up her sleeve, a tangible cue to herself to uphold her composure. She sat upright, her attention focused, unsure of how to respond.

Quietly, she scanned the faces of the other team members, seeking a glimmer of support or understanding, but all she received were blank stares. Their anticipation was palpable, and they waited for her to validate Frans's comment with an angry response.

Summoning her strength, she turned towards Greg, her eyes locked with his. "If everyone agrees with Frans, I am happy to respond. But, if not, it sounds like a personal complaint to me," she declared, her voice steady but laced with a hint of defiance. Her gaze remained fixed on Greg, silently challenging him as the team leader.

Greg broke the silence. "You are right, Thando," he replied, his voice softened by the situation. "Does anyone have anything to add? If you agree with Frans, please speak up. If not, I will excuse everyone. We will reconvene at dinner. I ask Frans and Thando to remain in the room."

The room grew still as the rest of the team evacuated, leaving Thando, Frans, and Greg alone. They remained seated, each person seemingly distant from one another. Greg could see the tense faces and decided to move closer between Thando and Frans. Positioning himself in a way that conveyed support, he turned to Thando, giving her the floor to speak. It was as if the entire discussion rested on the moment.

Thando took a deep breath, her emotions tightly wound within her. She mustered the strength to address the issue, her voice laced with vulnerability. "Can you please give me more examples where I have been "angry" during meetings?"

"I don't mean to label you as 'angry.' It's more about how your delivery might come across as forceful or intimidating to the rest of the team. I believe the team feels the same way."

Greg, known for his direct and matter-of-fact leadership style, sought to clarify the comment, "Let's stick to your opinion for clarity. However, we must address this issue based on facts, not assumptions or perceptions."

"So, you are intimidated by Thando's demeanor, Frans?

Thando admired Greg's straightforward approach, which she believed was influenced by his Dutch culture and commitment to fairness.

Having lived in different countries, he held on to his Dutch heritage's fundamental values and customs. Greg's heavy Dutch accent added a distinct charm to his words when the conversation intensified.

With its unique accent, his voice carried authority and authenticity, drawing Thando and others further into the discussion. Each word resonated with the richness of his cultural background, making his points more convincing.

" Can you provide specific examples of when Thando's delivery displayed unprofessional anger and adversely impacted our results?" his heavy Dutch accent continued delving into the matter, his voice growing weightier as the conversation intensified.

Leaning back in his chair, his face flushing red, Frans couldn't believe that he had unintentionally let slip his personal opinion of Thando in front of the entire team. His hushed words sank in, and he hesitated before responding. "Well, it's not necessarily about the results themselves. It's more about Thando's delivery and how she expresses herself."

The room breathed as Frans's words settled in everyone's awareness.

Thando sat resolutely in her chair, facing a colleague who was brazenly expressing his dislike for her. It felt to her as though her presence, her personality, was dissected and discussed as if she were an object to be analyzed. It was a disheartening experience for Thando.

She clenched her fists, desperately suppressing the anger and disappointment inside her. Every word spoken and intonation felt like a potential weapon aimed at her.

Summoning her courage, Thando finally broke her silence, her voice trembling with frustration." I heard you say that my work and results are not the issue, but you have a problem with how I speak." It was a bold declaration, a moment of reclaiming her voice in the face of dismissal and judgment.

Maintaining a calm but determined demeanor, Greg addressed Frans again, pushing for a response. "Frans, can you confirm if what Thando said is correct? We need to find a solution to communicate effectively with the rest of the team. And it seems to me that this issue is personal. It would be best if we resolve it quickly without involving too many people."

"Greg, I agree that this is a personal matter Frans has with me. It has undermined my professional integrity in front of the team. One of my requests is a public apology from Frans, or else we can involve H.R.," Thando asserted with a firm tone, mindful of her response and reluctant to unleash her full fury.

Frans responded with a contemptuous look, indicating his resistance to Thando's demand. He knew he had backed himself into a difficult position with no easy way out of her request. "I think that's a fair request. It's key to clarify that this observation is personal and unrelated to performance. Frans, is that clear?" Greg addressed Frans.

Frans defensively replied, "Are you asking for a public apology? I simply shared my observation and have nothing to apologize for!"

"In that case, Greg, I will seek personal legal advice," Thando responded matter-of-factly, directing her statement toward Greg.

"Fine! Fine! It doesn't have to escalate to that point. I can correct my statement to the team. I suggest we do it during our closing session. Are we done?" Frans exclaimed, looking at Greg, eager to excuse himself from the tense atmosphere.

"Yes, we're done. Thando, are you okay with this arrangement? Do you think that we have reached a conclusive solution?" Greg asked, shifting his attention to Thando.

After hearing Frans ' condescending response, Thando let out an involuntary deep sigh, enveloped with frustration and resignation. She was certain that she was fighting for an apology, respect, and acceptance. "Yes, we have a resolution. The apology during the closing meeting will suffice," she replied, closing her notebook and reaching for her bag, ready to wrap up the meeting.

*

Thando hurriedly dashed towards her room as if a swarm of bees were chasing after her. She avoided making eye contact with her colleagues, who were casually puffing away on their cigarettes outside the conference building on her path to the guest rooms. When she finally reached the sanctuary of her room, tears streamed down her face uncontrollably.

She swung open the door, and unfamiliar emotions met her, flooding her body and clouding her mind. It was a jumble of seething anger, shame, hurt, frustration, and disappointment, all swirling. She felt overwhelmed, not knowing where to begin or which emotion to tackle first. She could only surrender to her tears, letting them flow freely.

After an hour of crying and a heartfelt call to Harold, she composed herself, putting on her favorite Arabian perfume as a symbolic way to show her resilience. She remembered her invisible armor at this particular time, reminding herself not to let emotional battles at the upcoming dinner event break her. Looking at herself in the mirror, she spoke with grit, saying, "I won't hide my true self to make others happy. I won't let them destroy me."

*

On the last day of the conference, Greg, looking exhausted with a sunburn on his forehead, expressed gratitude to the team for organizing an amazing team-building weekend. Their goal of motivating the teams and fostering camaraderie among different business units had been successfully achieved. The atmosphere buzzed with energy and excitement, marking the event as a resounding success.

Taking advantage of the moment, Greg turned to each manager in the room, seeking their feedback on the event and whether its goals had been met. As he approached Frans, he halted, crossing his arms and prompting Frans to share any additional thoughts.

Thando, sitting up on her chair, became more attentive and nervous and started to manifest sweat. She couldn't ignore the heat rising in the back of her neck. After a moment of silence, Frans cleared his throat and turned his chair towards Thando.

"Thando, I misunderstood your feedback in the last meeting. I didn't mean to offend you," Frans admitted.

Greg interjected, wanting to keep things concise without delving into the details, and demanded, "Frans, please be clear!" He wanted to tell the team that such comments or behaviors would not be tolerated in the future.

Frans muttered, "I apologize for implying you're an angry person," without further explaining or mentioning the specific meetings Thando hoped he would address. She knew she wouldn't get more than that and accepted it. The room fell into an uncomfortable silence, and all eyes were on Thando, waiting for her response.

Thando breaks the tension by accepting Frans's apology, stating, "Apology accepted, Frans. We are one team, and let's continue delivering great results."

Greg was relieved when he realized that Thando wasn't entirely satisfied with the apology, so he expressed approval towards her, his face lighting up like a proud father, followed by a subtle nod as if to say, "You've handled it well."

*

The sun dipped low on the horizon as the team made their way to the buses, their laughter and chatter heard across the hotel hallways. The day had been a twist of adventure and camaraderie, and they boarded the buses with their luggage in tow. The memories of their epic obstacle courses echoed in their animated stories.

The bus turned into a lively place, with laughter and memories flying around like colorful confetti. Each tale brought to life the funny moments and triumphs they had experienced together. One memory stood out: a team member had been hit so hard by a rogue volleyball that they couldn't get up until the match ended. The whole team burst into laughter, finding the situation hilariously absurd.

The day's highlight was Greg's daring bet with another team leader. Instead of drinking tequila shots, he chose to stay covered in mud. The sight of him, all muddy and grinning, brought pure delight to everyone. It was a moment of freedom and rebellion, where the management team let loose and embraced the carefree spirit of the event.

Thando was fully engaged in the lively discussions, her eyes sparkling with joy as she relished the shared laughter and celebration. At that moment, she felt an undeniable sense of belonging among her teammates. The bonds they had formed during the day's escapades were stronger than ever.

Although she sensed that some of the other members of the management team were still puzzled by Frans's apology's context, Thando didn't worry about it. She knew that the respect she received from her team was genuine, and that mattered more to her than any fleeting moment of popularity.

The bus pulled away, and Thando felt a rush of sweet victory. She savored the sense of respect, holding onto it like a prized possession. She didn't need everyone to grasp every detail of the situation; she simply craved recognition and appreciation for her efforts.

IV. BETTING ON THE BOSS

Thando intuitively understood that going through different managers with diverse management styles would be an inevitable part of her career. Having grown into a resilient and determined individual, she had already embraced the art of shape-shifting and playing chameleon when adapting to different management styles.

It was like second nature to her. She attributed her adaptability to her survival instinct of code-switching. She knew how to crack the code and adjust her approach to fit in with the prevailing Western culture in the office. She knew how to shed her authentic self every time she walked into the building. As the trailblazer in her family, being the first to work in an office and travel internationally, she had learned how to navigate uncharted territories without a predefined roadmap. To her surprise, her deliberate inauthenticity gave her favorable results.

Over the years, Thando's career flourished, but at a cost. A 32-year-old single woman with no children, she quickly became a candidate of choice, making it easy for her to move between jobs. Her managers valued her flexibility: she didn't have to leave early to pick up kids, come in late due to doctor's appointments, or take many sick days. That allowed her to be readily available for business trips, impromptu travel, and late nights grabbing drinks with the boys. Thando honed her skills, gaining valuable experience, and her reputation began to spread, earning her recognition and respect within her industry.

Her success and professional standing grew, but her personal life remained untouched.

Her commitment to quality work and drive to deliver results made her a sought-after professional. In the boardrooms of bustling cities and the meeting rooms of multinational corporations, Thando adopted a subtly restrained demeanor. Replacing her vivacious gestures with more composed demeanors, her laughter muted to a polite chuckle. She created her secret passport to the land of professionalism, where self-expression was carefully curated, and emotions were kept under lock and key. She navigated the world gracefully, seamlessly blending in with the dominant corporate culture. Desperate to fit in and be accepted, she made the painful decision to remove her signature braids and straighten her hair. She hoped that conforming to societal expectations would make her more "acceptable" in the eyes of those around her. It was a soul-crushing compromise, surrendering to the pressure to assimilate.

Code-switching became an unavoidable price to pay for her career advancement. An unavoidable companion for Thando, an ever-present reminder of the sacrifices that needed to be made in her relentless pursuit of equality.

First, she tackled her accent, honing a more "Caucasian-sounding" speech pattern. She said goodbye to the richness of her natural intonations as she molded her voice to fit the mold. Then came the wardrobe transformation, bidding farewell to the vibrant colors and patterns that once defined her style and instead opting for the monotonous sea of black and blues. Even her taste buds weren't spared when she reluctantly traded her beloved pickled fish and achaar for the oh-so-proper cucumber sandwiches. Whichever way she looked at her path, it required sacrifices upon sacrifices.

But, oh, the contrast when Thando reunited with Lala and her beloved family! She reveled in the freedom to let her true self shine in those treasured moments. Among her trusted confidants, her infectious laughter echoed, her gestures became more animated, and her expressions exuded a vibrant energy. There was no need to censor her thoughts or stifle her emotions. Thando felt free to be as expressive and casual as she pleased, basking in the warmth of acceptance, surrounded by smiles and understanding nods. There, in the comforting embrace, she found relief from the pressures of her professional life, reconnecting with the joy of simply being herself.

On quiet days, she questioned the necessity of the change and sacrifice she needed to make for her identity to be accepted. But she quickly pushed the thought aside, knowing she had to keep moving forward. She'd done that throughout her childhood, and now, as an adult, she was grappling with the same issue, albeit in a different form.

It was in these contrasting spaces —the manicured, sometimes pretentious world of her career and the authentic warmth of her loved ones—that Thando discovered the full spectrum of her identity. She learned to navigate these dual worlds gracefully, straddling between the two worlds and adapting when needed, but always cherishing the moments of authenticity when she could let her spirit soar freely.

But there was one bitter pill Thando struggled to swallow: the concept of subjecting herself to a "boss" challenged her at every level of her career growth. While she worked well with managers who understood she thrived on results, not flattery, some focused more on her behavior toward them than on her deliverables.

Within the office walls and amongst her management peers, rumors filled the air, carrying tales of individuals sacrificing their time, energy, and even their essence in a desperate attempt to impress "The Boss." Ambitions soared, and unyielding dedication knew no bounds as employees pursued the elusive favor of their superior.

*

Friday mornings meant one thing: 8:30 a.m. executive meetings. Thando straightened her blazer, smoothing the wrinkles as she approached the boardroom. Five executive team members were seated, each reporting to the CEO. Thando, the Head of the Analyst Business Unit, was the only woman on the team, a fact that had her bracing for the usual "boys' club" banter and macho talk.

The chatter inside carried through the closed door, a reminder of the dynamics she'd grown accustomed to. It didn't bother her much, but Vusi's behavior annoyed her. As the head of Communications, Vusi, a fellow Black executive, was more interested in sucking up to The Boss than in supporting Thando, despite both being black and their sharing a similar cultural background. Sure, he'd chat with her in Zulu - their native language, but when it came time to back her up, he quickly threw her under the bus.

The contrast was striking; her white male colleagues showed her more acceptance and support than Vusi. On one occasion when Thando proposed an innovative strategy to streamline communication between their departments, Vusi, with his heavy private school accent, scoffed, claiming it was impractical and would only create confusion. He reiterated that each unit should remain autonomous, effectively dismissing Thando's plan. Later, he enthusiastically pitched a similar idea with a slightly different name, gaining The Boss's approval.

Thando's stomach tightened at the thought of enduring another meeting where she'd have to compromise her integrity. She dug her nails into her palm, remembering all the times she'd bitten her tongue, nodding against her better judgment. Could she keep climbing the ladder without losing herself? Her reflection in the glass door reminded her of the battles she'd fought to get here. She sighed heavily, pulled her shoulders back, and stepped inside.

In the boardroom, Vusi nodded eagerly at every word from The Boss, grinning as he offered to arrange brunches for their wives. Thando's fingers curled into a fist, her knuckles whitening. She understood the drive for progress, but Vusi's eagerness made her uneasy.

Thando shifted in her seat, her mind reverting to Vusi's attitude toward her and other Black women. He frequently dismissed their ideas in team meetings, rolling his eyes or interrupting their presentations. Even now, his eyes gleamed with a desperate hunger as he agreed with The Boss's every word, reinforcing the impression that his marriage to a mixed-race woman exaggerated his sense of superiority. Thando's stomach twisted, her heart sinking, realizing the conversation wasn't about plans or strategies but appeasing one person's whims. She exhaled slowly, the bitter taste of compromise heavy on her tongue.

*

Thando sat in her office, her face pale and her hands trembling. She'd just been fired, and though she had seen it coming, the sting was still fresh. The news hit hard, her mind replaying how her career had crumbled at the hands of "The Boss" and Vusi. The company's efficient hierarchy masked an uglier reality: decisions flowed with little regard for fairness or equity.

The office rattled with rumors, and Thando could almost hear Vusi's disdain as he labeled her "difficult." The accusation came as no surprise; Vusi had always sought to undermine her, treating her as an obstacle to be removed. But the final blow came from an unexpected direction.

Johno, a white subordinate, accused her of sexual harassment after a 1:1 lunch, twisting the reason for their meeting into a narrative of impropriety. Thando felt her blood boil learning about the accusation, but before she could defend herself, she was swiftly suspended, her authority dismissed in favor of her subordinate's voice.

Shockwaves rippled through the company and spilled over to industry associates, revealing the persistent influence of racial and gender dynamics. The incident accentuated the worthlessness of diversity programs, which seemed more like marketing tools than genuine efforts at inclusivity.

Thando's experience showed how her industry and the corporate space struggled to move beyond tokenism, forcing her to negotiate a careful path between her job's demands and the need for representation.

She had felt the reality of racial discrimination seep into her life in subtle, stealthy ways. At first, she thought she was overthinking it, the microaggressions less blatant than the clear racism she'd grown accustomed to. No one cursed at her threw stones, or openly shunned her, but people were cordial without warmth, and she felt the distance in their interactions. She swallowed the microaggressions, dismissing them as minor irritations, trying to focus on her work. But when she was packing up her office, the taste of injustice made her bitter. For Thando, it was not just another personal setback but a revelation of the systemic biases still lurking in the corporate sphere.

Adding to the controversy, whispers circulated about the company's internal incident handling. Some murmured that Thando's firing was a convenient way to silence her growing influence, while others hinted at The Boss's discomfort with her outspokenness. Vusi's closeness to 'The Boss' fueled rumors of a backroom deal, with speculation that Thando's suspension was orchestrated to consolidate Vusi's position.

Thando's resolve hardened. The corporate world had revealed its true nature, where representation and justice were challenges to overcome rather than guaranteed rights. She packed her belongings, feeling weighed down but determined, knowing it was just the start of a larger struggle.

*

Thando stood at a career crossroads, unemployed and drained of energy, after trying every possible strategy to overcome the systematic obstacles blocking her path.

She had still not reached out to her mentor and was desperate. She thought of the missed opportunity. Initially, reaching out to Mrs. Kala seemed like the perfect solution, sparking a burst of enthusiasm after a visit from her grandmother filled her with ideas and possibilities. However, that initial excitement faded as time passed, and Thando hesitated to take the next steps. Weeks turned into months, and she hadn't progressed or followed up with Mrs. Kala as intended.

Haunted by regret. Thando recognized that her hesitation and lack of action had become her barriers, walls she had unintentionally built around her ambitions.

She was still learning that asking for help was not a sign of weakness but a demonstration of her commitment to grow and improve.

With a deep breath, Thando reached out to Mrs. Kala, hoping their connection remained strong and that Mrs. Kala would offer her support once more.

She composed the email, Thando admitted to her past hesitation and shared her struggles honestly. She expressed her genuine desire to overcome the obstacles in her path and highlighted the importance of Mrs. Kala's guidance. Thando understood the value of transparency in her journey towards growth.

Though embarrassed by the delay, Thando chose honesty and took responsibility for her actions. She wanted to show her seriousness about positively changing her life and career.

In her email to Mrs. Kala, Thando expressed her genuine admiration and respect. She didn't hold back, sharing her struggles and aspirations with vulnerability. Thando's words weren't just empty pleas for help; they were heartfelt expressions of her earnest desire to learn and grow. With every sentence, she revealed her deep understanding of the value Mrs. Kala's guidance could bring to her journey. Thando approached the opportunity with an open heart and a genuine readiness to absorb whatever wisdom Mrs. Kala had to offer.

*

With more time on her hands following her sudden dismissal, Thando dedicated herself to reading and contemplating her next steps. While perusing her usual business news, she stumbled upon an article that immediately seized her attention. It detailed Mrs. Kala's recent promotion to Senior Business Executive, overseeing expansion projects in Africa and Europe. The article vividly portrayed Mrs. Kala's new role, managing a team of over 30 branches and navigating challenges from a demanding board of directors. It didn't hesitate to praise her achievements, dubbing her "The First Black Woman to be offered a partnership with a Multinational" for the positive changes she'd instigated within her company. Intrigued, Thando absorbed every detail, finding inspiration in Mrs. Kala's journey as she considered her path.

Pleasantly surprised by Mrs. Kala's prompt response, Thando and her mentor agreed to meet the following Friday. Mrs. Kala, having previously worked with Vusi and "The Boss," had already caught wind of Thando's circumstances and was prepared to step in and offer her support.

Thando arrived at the bustling restaurant, a favorite spot among executives for its refined ambiance and secluded corners ideal for confidential discussions. The soft hum of chatter and gentle background music wrapped her, almost like a soundtrack to her swirling emotions. Thando was doing her best to maintain composure; her struggles bore down on her as she braced herself for the meeting with Mrs. Kala.

She spotted Mrs. Kala in the elegant ambiance of the restaurant. She was an elegant woman in her early fifties, with natural short hair framing her face. Unlike the flashy appearance often seen in high-profile figures, Mrs. Kala opted for a more relaxed style without any makeup. With her poised demeanor, Mrs. Kala exuded warmth in her eyes, making Thando feel like conversing with a strict yet understanding mother figure.

Thando and Mrs. Kala settled into their seats across from each other. Thando felt a flood of emotions threatening to gush out. Against her efforts to maintain a composed facade, she could sense her inner turmoil betraying her. Mrs. Kala, ever perceptive, greeted her with warmth, her eyes reflecting a deep understanding of Thando's struggles.

Without hesitation, Mrs. Kala reached out and cocooned Thando in a comforting embrace. Thando's facade crumbled at that moment, and the tears she had held back for months finally broke free, rushing down her cheeks. It was a cathartic release, the culmination of months of pent-up emotions.

For Thando, the moment was a revelation. In her naïve pursuit of success, she had neglected her emotional well-being.

Reaching across the table, Mrs. Kala gently clasped Thando's hand and whispered, "Your feelings are completely valid, and you're not alone in this. It's natural to feel hurt by such unfair treatment. What you're going through is sexism and racism. Your boss, whether intentionally or not, is treating you in a way that's not okay." Her words were a soothing balm to Thando's frayed nerves,

Thando's heart raced as she absorbed Mrs. Kala's words. It was a moment of clarity, recognizing the countless instances where she had felt belittled and undervalued. Finally, someone understood the underlying forces chipping away at her self-esteem.

"There are two valid things to consider," Mrs. Kala continued, her voice steady with determination. "Firstly, your boss's racist actions not only affect your mental well-being but also undermine the valuable contributions you bring to the team. The behavior must be addressed, and you need legal support."

Mrs. Kala empathized with Thando's fear, knowing the daunting prospect of taking on a big corporation. She encouraged her to confront her boss, detailing the specific instances and their impact. Though there might be defensiveness, Mrs. Kala assured Thando that her feelings were valid.

"But I've already been fired. How will this help?" Thando's voice quivered with anxiety as her deepest fear surfaced.

Mrs. Kala nodded solemnly. "Everything must be handled with a lawyer from now on. Any reasons for your dismissal must be properly documented based on your performance or evidence of the incident you're being accused of. If unjust actions were taken against you, you have every right to pursue legal action, and I strongly recommend you do so. Also, consider taking legal action against that Johno boy. I suspect they all conspired together. Address them all with legal action, but sue each individually."

"Even Vusi?" Thando interjected, hoping for a different response.

Thando listened intently, feeling the weight of the conversation settling on her nerves. "I understand," she replied, realizing the seriousness of the situation.

Mrs. Kala continued, offering her guidance. "Take your time before setting up the meeting. Frame your message carefully and use the company's policies to guide your conversation. Highlight any progress made in racial inclusion within the company as examples."

Thando nodded gratefully. "Thank you so much," she said, her relief palpable.

Mrs. Kala's tone was measured by switching topics, which is another crucial aspect of Thando's situation.

"Make sure your job performance results are up to scratch," she advised, her voice carrying a note of caution. If other tactics don't work, they may try to make you look like a poor performer. I hope you were documenting everything."

Thando absorbed the advice, recognizing the importance of safeguarding her professional achievements amidst the turmoil she faced.

"But in the future, never put the fate of your career in the hands of any boss," Mrs. Kala warned.

"Maybe his wallet, " she continued with laughter filling the room. Thando couldn't help but smile, grateful for her mentor's ability to infuse humor into their serious discussions. Moments like these made their conversations truly enriching.

Mrs. Kala's feedback underscored the level of responsibility Thando held in managing her career. Her words were direct and clear, leaving no room for misinterpretation.

"It's wise not to fully rely on your boss to advance your career or identify opportunities that fit your strengths," Mrs. Kala advised, her wisdom shining through. "Take control of the situation instead of waiting to be given instructions. Your relationship with your manager is your responsibility. Be productive and efficient in your job, and your contributions will be acknowledged."

Thando felt empowered by Mrs. Kala's guidance. Here was someone who treated her as an accomplished professional, regardless of her background or circumstances.

"You're working with your boss, not for your boss," Mrs. Kala emphasized, punctuating her point with a raised index finger. Thando nodded in agreement, fully embracing the wisdom imparted to her.

Thando left the breakfast meeting feeling seen, acknowledged, and validated. Mrs. Kala's guidance provided her with a clear perspective on her circumstances. Driving through the bustling streets on her way to her mother's house in Thembisa, she found solace in the familiar lines of Mr. Useni's inspiring poem. Reciting it aloud in the car, she allowed the words to resonate deep within her soul.

"Hey, black girl," she whispered, aware of the strength of those simple words:
"Do you know you are strong?
I mean strong.
Do you know what you can do?
what do you want to do
if you try to do what you can do?"

*

Three weeks after their impactful breakfast meeting, Thando's inbox chimed with an email from Mrs. Kala. As she read the subject line, excitement, and curiosity rushed through her, returning memories of their meaningful conversation that day.

In the email, Mrs. Kala began by expressing her gratitude to Thando for sharing her story openly and honestly. She admired Thando's ambition to pursue her dreams against all the challenges she faced. The warmth in Mrs. Kala's words acknowledged the strength it takes to persevere through life's obstacles.

Thando continued reading, drawn into Mrs. Kala's career journey. With eloquence, Mrs. Kala recounted the struggles and triumphs she had experienced throughout her life. She shared instances where she had faced situations similar to Thando's and how she navigated them with resilience and grace. Each anecdote vividly depicted courage and resilience, leaving Thando inspired and hopeful.

In her email, Mrs. Kala didn't just provide advice; she engaged with Thando personally, creating a deep connection between them. The email offered practical tips, life lessons, and uplifting words that Thando knew she could turn to whenever she needed guidance.

"I believe in you, Thando," Mrs. Kala wrote, her confidence in her abilities shining through every word. Remember that your dreams are worth seeing the light of day, and difficulties are just there to course correct."

Whispers of the saga reached the ears of the press, and Thando braced herself for the storm that was about to unfold. Reporters began reaching out to the company, eager to uncover the truth behind the controversy. The evidence in Thando's favor was undeniable, prompting the Vice President to arrange a meeting with her to discuss a resolution before the situation escalated further.

In the negotiation room, Thando sat with her shoulders slumped. Her usually confident demeanor was replaced by a weariness that created lines of exhaustion on her face. Each breath she took seemed heavier than the last as if she were carrying the weight of the world on her shoulders.

Even with the fatigue evident in her eyes, a flicker of determination refused to be extinguished. It was a quiet resolve, buried beneath layers of uncertainty and fatigue, but present nonetheless.

With every word spoken in the room, she pushed herself to maintain her composure, to keep her emotions.

In those tense moments, Mrs. Kata's lawyer, who also became Thando's Lawyer, stood beside her, a silent pillar of support during the typhoon of negotiations.

The Vice President proposed a settlement to avoid public disclosure, recognizing the potential damage it could inflict on the company's reputation. Thando, hesitant to return to her previous role, saw an opportunity for a win-win solution. She agreed to consult for a year to assist in revamping the company's diversity program, accepting the settlement package offered, which included stock options.

Reflecting on the inequality that persisted in society, particularly in education, Thando understood the importance of her journey. She was often the only woman of her race in meetings, navigating challenges unique to her experience. The incident became a personal mission for Thando, motivating her to pave the way for future generations.

*

Thando, a seasoned professional, had spent countless years navigating the ins and outs of the corporate world. Over time, it did not matter how successful she was. Race, gender, and cultural biases still mattered to her executives and associates more than her merits.

Understanding the significance of her Diversity & Inclusion role, Thando prioritized diversity and inclusion. When hiring new college graduates, she eagerly joined the panel, determined to ensure diversity remained a focal point in the selection process.

*

Thando and Trudie set up their collaborative workspace in a cozy corner of the office, a small boardroom not used by the main office. The walls were adorned with colorful posters and inspirational quotes, creating a vibrant atmosphere that sparked creativity and innovation.

Twice a week, they met in a small office across the main building, surrounded by the comforting hum of their computers and the soft glow of desk lamps. Papers were strewn across the table, filled with scribbled ideas and brainstorming notes.

Thando and Trudie developed mutual respect and engaged in lively discussions. Their voices echoed off the walls as they debated strategies and solutions. They poured over research findings and case studies, drawing inspiration from their own experiences and those shared by their colleagues.

Their collaboration seamlessly blended Thando's strategic vision and Trudie's practical expertise. Thando's pain was birthing her purpose. Together, they crafted a roadmap for success, outlining clear objectives and actionable steps to foster a more inclusive workplace environment.

From mentorship programs to cultural sensitivity training, every aspect of their program was carefully designed to empower employees and new hires and create growth opportunities. As the year drew to a close, so did their contract. They put the finishing touches on their project.

They had created something truly impactful, something that would benefit the company and make a difference in the lives of their colleagues. As they prepared to launch their program, Thando and Trudie knew they were taking a significant stride toward fostering a more inclusive tomorrow. Thando's time at the company had not been in vain.

The new hire training and welcome included the following recommendations:

The new hire training and welcome included the following recommendations:

Document Your Progress: Record your achievements, including positive feedback, successful projects, and instances of bias or discrimination. The documentation can help you advocate for yourself effectively and address concerns with HR or management.

Communicate Your Strengths: Focus on highlighting shared goals and interests when interacting with colleagues. By emphasizing common ground, you can integrate into the team smoothly and identify potential instances of exclusion to seek support if needed.

Manage Your Emotions: Recognize and understand the emotions that arise when discussing diversity-related topics. Be aware of how gratitude or stress may influence your responses, ensuring you express yourself effectively and navigate discussions clearly.

Avoidance: Acknowledge the company's diversity goals and embrace your role in promoting diversity and inclusion. Avoiding discussions about your inclusion in a diversity program hinders your career growth. Embrace your unique perspective to establish yourself within the company and seize growth opportunities.

Through her experience, Thando learned the importance of fostering an encouraging atmosphere for people from varied backgrounds to be recognized for their unique skills, abilities, and potential rather than being token symbols of inclusivity.

Through her experience, Thando learned the importance of fostering an encouraging atmosphere for people from varied backgrounds to be recognized for their unique skills, abilities, and potential rather than being token symbols of inclusivity.

*

That night, Thando tossed and turned under her sheets, her body buzzing like a live wire. Next to her lay Mr. Caramel, a friendly acquaintance she had met during a lively night out with Trudie and a few friends, his presence warm but not imposing. Steering clear of relationship expectations, Thando kept her interactions with men light and casual, savoring the freedom to pursue her goals.

Her mind raced like a whirring pinwheel, replaying every exhilarating moment of the final Diversity project. The project's completion had released a torrent of emotions, making sleep feel out of reach. She felt like a child on Christmas Eve, excited to unpack her new Sunday best dress. Mr. Useni Eugene Perkins' poem danced in her mind, its comforting rhythm infusing her with renewed purpose, bringing her dreams closer than ever. Her pain had birthed a purpose that would continue to serve others even after she left the company.

And then there was Mrs. Kala, giving her wisdom and encouragement. Thando's heart expanded, knowing she was not alone, with supportive mentors lighting her path.

V. Trailblazer or Token: The First Black Woman to……

Deep within Thando's mind, a seed of suspicion flourished into a belief that colored her worldview. Her personal experience supported her theory. In her worldview, the corporate landscape was more of a battlefield where powerful unseen forces worked to maintain control. She saw it as a system that favored and elevated Caucasian men, with a carefully orchestrated strategy designed to create chaos and marginalize minority groups.

Certain company departments stood out to her as chaotic breeding grounds for hopeful interns from affirmative action programs. Thando saw these programs as traps, with ambitious young black women walking into them unaware. Roles in the Services, Marketing, Finance, and Human Resources Departments were created to foster an illusion of inclusivity that was intentionally vague and lacked proper training and resources. These roles lured in driven candidates, who soon found themselves in a rigged system designed to frustrate and exhaust them.

Thando believed the setup aimed to unfairly blame these individuals, turning them into symbols of failure and perpetuating a narrative of incompetence among black women. The narrative then justified bringing in another Caucasian person for a prominent position to "fix" the failure. The outlook consumed Thando, shaping her interactions and perspective.

Thando's belief in the cunning system encouraged her resolve, and she escaped through books.

Books became her trusted weapons, helping her navigate the complexities of her world. Early in her professional journey, Thando realized the limitations her upbringing had placed on her. Sports were restricted by lack of funding, the books available were carefully selected by the government to shape her social class, and travel felt like an unattainable luxury because every penny she earned went towards necessities.

In her harsh reality, reading was her lifeline.

During her business travels, she would pass time idly flipping through business magazines. One day, her eyes settled on a cover story celebrating a black woman's rise to a senior position. The headline announced,

"The First Black Woman to..." and the article detailed her journey, outlining her trials and triumphs.

A familiar tightness gripped Thando's chest. At first, there was a glimmer of pride, but it quickly gave way to a wave of conflicting emotions. The article framed the woman's success as a remarkable anomaly, overlooking her accomplishments and focusing instead on her identity as a black woman. Thando sensed the subtle cynicism lurking in the words. The heavy undertone conveyed that even though the achievement was significant, it was noteworthy primarily because it was accomplished by a black person.

The narrative reinforced the idea that people of color remained outsiders, even as they made strides, casting a shadow over individual achievements. Frustration simmered inside Thando, her hand tightening around the magazine. To her, these stories felt like carefully selected exaggerations, presenting a facade of progress while concealing the harsh realities that persisted. The narrative weighed on her, making her dream of gracing a business magazine cover enticing and daunting, knowing the recognition might come tinged with the same cynicism.

"How many talented people have persevered through the same grueling journey and received no recognition for their remarkable achievements because of timing or discrimination in their industries?" she thought.

The question in her head stimulated her curiosity further.

"Is the bar set so unattainably high for a person of color that every accomplishment becomes a groundbreaking feat?" she questioned, a tinge of frustration creeping into her thoughts.

"Are the odds stacked against me from the start, making success an elusive dream?"

Though she held deep convictions about the cunning nature of the corporate system, her unwavering desire to be featured on a cover persisted.

Rather than dampening her ambition, the realization further hastened her goal to see the top.

*

Thando sat across from Trudie in a cozy corner of the café, her hands wrapped around a steaming cup of tea. The warmth soothed her, but her thoughts remained tangled. Sensing her friend's unease, Trudie leaned forward, her brow furrowing as she spoke.

"Thando," Trudie began, her voice tinged with curiosity and concern, "what kind of headlines would you like to see?"

Before Thando could reply, Trudie launched into a passionate monologue, her words flowing with conviction. "Media outlets controlled by those in power tend to be selective," she asserted, leaning forward earnestly. "Black folks need to tell their own stories, from their perspectives. It's about owning the narrative."

"When did you start using American lingo like Folks " Thando teased Trudie and listened intently, nodding in agreement as Trudie continued.

"By guiding and shaping the storytelling process," Trudie emphasized, "you can ensure there is no misrepresentation. People will feel empowered to share the complete story, giving a true picture of their background and what their experiences truly mean to them. The truth must be told by those who have lived it."

Trudie's sincerity was evident, her determination to defend the need for free speech and for journalists to shape headlines evident in every word. Thando absorbed her friend's perspective, considering the power of narrative control in reshaping societal perceptions.

Thando absorbed Trudie's words, considering their implications. "I agree," she added, "but we must also acknowledge the countless untold stories of black success. Not every breakthrough gets the spotlight it deserves."

She sighed, feeling the weight of unspoken stories. "So while headlines like 'First black person to...' have their place," she concluded, "they often overshadow the many others who deserve recognition too."

Thando was no stranger to uncomfortable conversations, especially when it came to addressing issues of inequality. With Trudie, she dove into these discussions headfirst, without fear, knowing they both valued honesty above all else. Hours were spent dissecting the company's diversity program and navigating differing viewpoints, yet strangely, it only strengthened their bond. Thando and Trudie trusted each other to speak their minds authentically—a rare dynamic in their corporate environment.

Trudie's conviction struck a chord with both of them, stirring memories of an article Thando had read in a business magazine. It featured Viola Davis's powerful acceptance speech at the 2015 Emmy Awards, where she made history as the first African American actress to win Best Actress in a Drama Series. Viola's words echoed in Thando's mind as she recalled, "The only thing that separates women of color from anyone else is an opportunity. You cannot win an Emmy for roles that are simply not there." " It was a poignant reminder of the barriers people of color face in industries with limited opportunities.

Thando couldn't shake the significance of Viola's speech, realizing it extended far beyond the entertainment industry. It spoke to any field where black individuals were not the dominant majority. They were constantly burdened with the expectation of being trailblazers, breaking ground in spaces that had previously overlooked their talents. As Thando envisioned her future, Viola's words lingered in her thoughts.

Lost in contemplation, Thando let her imagination take flight for the rest of the day. She pictured the headlines of her that would one day adorn the front pages of prestigious business publications.

She envisioned "In Her League: Thandosizwe Dhladhla Redefines the Prize of Success for a Black Woman in the Corporate World," a testament to her unwavering dedication to reshaping the narrative and paving the way for others to follow.

VI. Time To Recharge

Thando and her boyfriend set off on their much-needed getaway to Kruger National Park, and she drifted back to her childhood days. Life was simpler then, with worries far from her mind. Ignoring the excitement of their trip, thoughts of work still hung heavy over her. They drove along, and Thando couldn't shake the responsibilities that came with her new role as Regional Director of a bank. Surrounded by the beauty of nature, she found moments of ease, reminding herself of the journey that had led her here. With each passing mile, she allowed herself to relax and unwind, grateful for the chance to unwind before charging back to endless meetings and deadlines.

"They say love is blind, but for Thando and Harold, it was also deafening. They met at a concert of their favorite music band in Brazil, both deciding to crowd-surf simultaneously. Their paths crossed mid-air, resulting in a head-on collision that sent them to the ground with a resounding thud. Stunned and bruised, they locked eyes, sharing an immediate connection even with the throbbing heads and the blaring music. Words seemed unnecessary because their smiles communicated effortlessly.

When Thando looked at Harold, she saw a man of striking presence. Standing tall at around 6 feet, he commanded attention with his confident demeanor and charismatic aura. His athletic build spoke of dedication to fitness, with well-defined muscles hinting at strength and vitality.

Harold's features were chiseled and rugged, drawing the eye with a strong jawline, high cheekbones, and a straight nose. Deep and expressive, his eyes held a magnetic quality that seemed to capture Thando's gaze effortlessly, conveying a wealth of emotions with a glance.

His hair, styled to enhance his masculine charm, framed his face with an allure that was impossible to ignore. Whether neatly groomed or slightly tousled, it only added to his overall attractiveness.

They quickly exchanged each other's mobile numbers and agreed to meet again after the show.

Thando's mind buzzed with thoughts, her imagination running wild with the possibilities of what she could do to Harold's body. With a mischievous grin spreading across her face, she felt excitement coursing through her veins.

In a frisky and playful mood, she decided to take matters into her own hands. Her fingers danced across her phone screen as she typed a teasing message to Harold. Each word was laced with a hint of seduction, her heart racing with anticipation as she hit send.

As she waited for his response, Thando couldn't help but chuckle at her boldness. The mere thought of Harold had ignited a fire within her, causing her to break out into a light sweat in the most unexpected places. It was a sensation both exhilarating and deliciously naughty, leaving her eagerly awaiting what the night might bring.

In that instance of forgetfulness, she couldn't recall his name and ended up calling him Charlie instead – the first random Caucasian name that popped into her head.

Intrigued by Thando's memory lapse, Harold couldn't resist the allure of the situation. He equally anticipated meeting her at the hotel's rooftop bar, surrounded by city lights.

On the rooftop, the atmosphere crackled with electric energy between them. The dimly lit bar intensified their intimate connection. Thando's mysterious smile and flirtatious glances drew Harold in, locking him in with her every move.

Harold's plan to leave the hotel was forgotten as the night progressed. He surrendered himself to the intoxicating pleasure of Thando's company. Drawn to Thando's enigmatic charm, they explored each other's physical desires and fantasies without limitations.

Their vacation days blurred into a whirlwind of passion and intimacy, leaving them yearning for more.

Harold introduced Thando to classical music and Limoncello making, activities that were staples in his family for generations. Thando, in return, shared with Harold the rhythms of kwaito and the spirited family gatherings that filled her childhood, vibrant with storytelling and laughter. Their exchanges went beyond mere cultural sharing; they were acts of love and acceptance, allowing each to enter the other's world with respect and curiosity.

Harold and Thando's relationship thrived even with the miles apart, with him living across the ocean in the bustling streets of America. Their deep connection went beyond the physical distance. Night after night, they engaged in long conversations about the nuances of race, the complexities of family life, and their future aspirations.

With every story and secret they shared, their bond grew stronger, each conversation pulling them closer, and the miles between them simply disappeared.

Harold became Thando's rock. He urged her to challenge society's norms and embrace her true self. His unwavering encouragement gave her the strength to break free from societal expectations and helped her embrace her uniqueness. Thando, in turn, gave Harold the space to sink deeper into his innermost self. He shed the facade of societal expectations to reveal his authentic essence. Together, they created a haven where they cherished vulnerability and fostered honesty.

*

During the trip, her mind drifted back to the vivid memories of her childhood, to that fateful day when she first stumbled upon the poem that forever molded her life's path. And even then, after all these years, the poem still resonated within her, as though Mr. Perkins had penned it exclusively for her.

Harold glanced over at her; concern etched his brow. "Are you doing all right over there?" he asked, his American accent still fresh.

Startled, Thando snapped back to reality and met his gaze. "Yes... I was just lost in my thoughts," she replied, her voice tinged with melancholy.

They drove through the stunning landscape. Thando's body was in the car, but her mind was still in the office. She wanted to relax and embrace the few precious days they had managed to secure away from the chaos of their careers. Still, the suffocating thought of the mountain of work waiting for her return sent waves of anxiety coursing through her body.

"I know I need to relax and enjoy this time off," Thando confessed, her voice betraying her inner struggle. "But it's hard for me to let go, knowing the pile of work waiting for me when we return."

Harold's eyes softened, and he squeezed her hand reassuringly. "You've worked tirelessly, Thando. You deserve this break," he said, his voice filled with conviction. "Your dedication and commitment are undeniable, and taking care of yourself doesn't diminish that in any way."

Just like the many incredible black women she witnessed around her, she had been raised to strive for excellence and surpass expectations. The thought of taking time off filled her with apprehension, fearing it might convey a message of falling short.

*

Harold and Thando stepped into the lively travel agency, their excitement for their long-awaited vacation to Kruger Park palpable. Their eyes met, childlike anticipation and relief reflecting in their gaze. Without saying a word, they shared an understanding: the trip would serve as a much-needed reprieve from the demanding pace of their work lives.

Approaching the counter, Harold's face lit up with a warm smile. He leaned in closer to Thando, a mischievous glint in his eye, and whispered, "Remember, no work talk allowed." His playful wink conveyed his effort to make their vacation a time of relaxation and connection.

Thando couldn't contain her laughter, a burst of joy that reverberated through the agency. She had become so consumed by pursuing success in the corporate world that she had forgotten the liberating feeling of truly letting go. The unnecessary stress of deadlines and endless meetings seemed to dissolve with Harold.

Their guide, Bennett, emanated warmth and wisdom, immediately sensing the electric connection between Harold and Thando. With an enchanting smile, he introduced himself, setting the stage for the captivating adventure that awaited them in the wild beauty of Kruger Park. Starting their journey, their driver to the Outlook Lodge in Benoni became a classroom. In the thick, bustling streets of Johannesburg, he effortlessly navigated through the evening traffic while enthralling them with his intricate knowledge of the city's geography, the historical significance of their route to Paul Kruger Gate, population densities, rainfall patterns, and a wealth of captivating trivia—all of it served as a delightful backdrop to their scenic drive through Benoni, even though Thando's fatigue prevented her from absorbing every detail.

Harold and Thando thoroughly enjoyed their stay at the Outlook Lodge, a delightful retreat filled with tranquility and peace. The lodge seamlessly blended contemporary and traditional African aesthetics in its architectural design. The use of earthy tones, thatched roofs, and spacious interiors created an inviting atmosphere that harmonized beautifully with the untamed wilderness beyond its borders.

Their bedroom exuded a soothing ambiance with its soft color palette of warm browns and creams, perfectly complementing the lodge's vibrant green surroundings. Although modest, it offered all the necessary amenities for a comfortable stay. With a television, coffee maker, kettle, two cozy beds, and a convenient cabinet, the room overlooked the scenic front lawn.

Having already satisfied their hunger during their journey, Thando and Harold settled into their room. They decided to skip dinner and instead take a stroll around the property. They wandered through the well-maintained grounds; the moonlit path was their guide, painting a dreamlike ambiance that mirrored their blossoming romance. They discovered inviting benches, a picturesque lake, and an array of lively birdlife, all adding to the lodge's charm and providing a visually captivating experience.

With soft touches and whispered expressions of affection, they succumbed to the comforting embrace of sleep.

After a delightful breakfast, Thando and Harold eagerly joined an older couple from the UK on their honeymoon for an adventurous day in the African bushveld. Their excitement grew when they met with their ranger, Robin, who would guide them through the wilderness.

At exactly 8:00 am, the group set off on their morning drive, with Robin leading the way in his trusty Land Rover. They ventured deeper into the wilderness; the midday sun beat down on them, intensifying the anticipation. Suddenly, around a bend in the dusty road, they spotted a magnificent sight: a group of four lionesses leisurely basking in the bushveld. The regal creatures seemed undisturbed by the presence of the small group of land rovers that had gathered on the opposite side of the road.

Unfazed by the spectators, one of the lionesses slowly rose to her feet, her eyes gleaming with curiosity. She cast a majestic gaze upon the captivated onlookers, inviting them to witness her wild world. With a graceful stretch, she started to prowl towards the group, her powerful muscles rippling beneath her golden coat.

Heartbeats quickened as Thando, Harold, and their fellow travelers watched in awe and trepidation. Robin, the seasoned guide, calmly reassured them that they were safe within the confines of the Land Rovers. The tension and excitement in the air were palpable as the lioness approached, her regal presence commanding respect.

As the lioness drew closer, a sudden rustling in the nearby thickets caught everyone's attention. Their eyes widened as a massive male lion emerged from the underbrush, the Lion's majestic mane flowing in the wind. He emitted a deep, rumbling growl that resonated through the savannah, making the ground vibrate beneath the tires of the Land Rovers.

The group held their breath, their hearts pounding in their chests, as the male Lion approached the lionesses. A moment of intense anticipation followed, and then, to everyone's amazement, the lionesses welcomed the male with affectionate rubs and gentle purrs. It was a rare and mesmerizing display of harmony and unity within the pride.

Captivated by the extraordinary wildlife encounter, Thando, Harold, and their newfound friends marveled at the raw beauty of nature unfolding before their eyes. They couldn't believe their luck in witnessing such an intimate moment between these powerful creatures.

The sun started going down, spreading cozy warmth over the savannah, and the lion pride slowly disappeared into the golden grasslands. The excited group continued their journey with Robin, eager to unravel more surprises hidden within the untamed wilderness.

*

Once back at camp, Thando and Harold reunited with the rest of their quirky group – the Riis-Vestergaards, a Danish couple who seemed to have a knack for getting lost in the wild. They had just arrived in Johannesburg, where Vagn, the husband, was preparing to conquer a company marathon. It was good that they met up with Thando and Harold, their trusted neighbors, who often relied on them to navigate their way back to their chalet in the absolute darkness of the bush.

After savoring a sumptuous feast, they gathered around, eager to share their tales of the day while indulging in a bottle or three of wine.

Vagn, the adventurous soul, regaled everyone with his wild escapades from the previous day. First, he recounted the exhilarating moment when he and Robin, armed with a camera, stumbled upon a majestic male elephant minding its own business and peacefully grazing when the moment escalated into an unexpected showdown when the bull charged towards them, causing Vagn's nerves to waver between laughter and terror over the following days.

In a stroke of sheer luck, Vagn witnessed a leopard in action, making an epic kill. It was the sighting that tourists would sell their souls for, and Vagn knew he had hit the wildlife jackpot. A triumphant grin spread across his face, knowing he had fulfilled a dream that wildlife enthusiasts wait a lifetime to witness.

The wine flowed, and so did the laughter and camaraderie. The group joked about the Danish couple's misadventures, teasing Vagn about his unexpected encounters with charging elephants and elusive leopards. It was a night filled with mirth and merriment, with tales that would be retold with exaggerated gusto for years.

*

The hours turned into days, and they soon discovered that the beginning of the year was surprisingly quiet in the African bush. The enthusiastic tourists who initially dreamt of an adventurous African safari quickly traded their bush-soaked ideals for the comfort of hotels, rental cars, and fancy dinners at John Dory's in the bustling city. Even the South Africans who had escaped to the wilderness for the holidays had no choice but to return to their jobs in those bustling cities. So, what remained at the camp were a handful of sunburned Swedish holidaymakers, accompanied by their energetic kids, and a bunch of random South Africans desperately hoping to spot a leopard.

The night before their final day in the bush, the ridiculously brainy lodge guide, who had welcomed Thando and Harold with a sign full of obscure facts and a brain bursting with knowledge about everything under the sun, would also be their designated driver back home.

Bright and early at 5:30 am, Bennett had them up and ready to roll as if he had secretly invented a caffeinated alarm clock. Nobody was thrilled about the early start, but after gulping gallons of fresh coffee, they begrudgingly loaded their gear into the lodge's rusty minibus they called the nickname Kambie, which Bennett had driven through the night. With the daylight gradually creeping in, they embarked on one last safari drive before the epic journey back home.

Cruising through the park, Thando felt an energy coursing through her veins. She was ready to conquer the world with her newfound passion for her job. She kicked her feet and marveled at the incredibly green landscape of Skukuza Lowveld passing by. The sun peeked out from between scattered clouds, remnants of a light rain shower they had enjoyed the previous evening.

In the distance, they spotted a baby elephant gracefully trailing behind its majestic herd. "Did you know that elephants have tongues that are as long as a giraffe's neck? "Bennett chimed in, unable to resist enlightening his captive audience. "I mean, imagine the baby elephant trying to blow up balloons for its birthday party!" he added, chuckling at the absurd image.

Thando, struggling to hold her, laughed back and added, "I guess it would be one heck of a party trick! Hey, Bennett, do you have any other mind-blowing animal facts up your sleeve?" she asked, intrigued.

Grinning mischievously, Bennett replied, "Oh, you bet! Did you know hippos can hold their breath for up to five minutes? Imagine challenging a hippo to a breath-holding contest at the community pool! Talk about an unfair advantage!"

The group erupted in laughter, still in high spirits from their wildlife adventure. The bush had not only filled their minds with breathtaking sights but also revived their humor. They continued their journey, exchanging fascinating and comical animal facts.

They neared the end of their journey; Thando glanced at Harold, her eyes brimming with unspoken love. Everything else faded away at that moment, leaving only the bond between them that mattered most.

With a tender smile, Harold reached out to gently cup Thando's face, his touch conveying a wealth of unspoken emotions. "This trip has been a revelation," he whispered,

"In your presence, I've rediscovered the true essence of what truly matters. You've awakened a fire within me.

Thando's heart fluttered, her breath catching as she realized the depth of Harold's revelation. "I also have clarity," she confessed, her voice trembling with vulnerability and gentleness. "This journey has shown me the beauty of our country, its flaws braided with its undeniable appeal. It has sparked something inside me, a burning desire to approach my career with fresh eyes, to forge a path that aligns with my deepest passions and values."

A flicker of admiration danced in Harold's eyes; his emotions swelled, and he couldn't contain his pride for his partner. "Adda girl, you are destined for greatness, my love," he whispered, his voice laced with conviction, wishing he could ease the social and racial injustices that Thando had endured.

Hey black child.
Do you know you are strong?
I mean strong.
Do you know what you can do?
What you want to do
If you try to do
What you can do

VII. Embracing Office Politics

Thando found deep resonance in the quote by Lance Armstrong, "Pain is temporary; quitting is forever." Whenever she faced challenging situations, she would recite empowering lines from her beloved poem to maintain emotional balance. The time she repeated the empowering mantra, "Do you know you can do what you want to do if you try to do what you can do."

When life became overwhelming, Thando had her ritual. She would retreat to the bathroom, facing herself in the mirror. Slowly, word by word, she would recite the empowering quotes. The mirror technique became her way of confronting her precarious circumstances head-on. Those memorized words served as a resounding reminder, urging her not to give in to the temptation of quitting.

She translated that mindset into everything she did. On one occasion, she insisted on baking a picture-perfect, multi-layered cake for Yaya's 30th birthday celebration.

Thando's kitchen was a battlefield. Flour dusted the countertops, sugar crystals sparkled on the floor, and broken eggshells littered the surface, crunching under her feet. During the chaos, she stood at the center, her apron streaked with butter and batter, holding a spatula like a battle-worn weapon. She glanced at the leaning tower of layers before her, each sliding precariously to the side, threatening to collapse into a sugary heap.

With a sigh, Thando caught a glimpse of her reflection on the oven door, her face smeared with chocolate and her hair dusted with flour. A started to spread across her face, but she bit it back, tightening her grip on the spatula. "I've got this," she muttered, her mantra spilling from her lips like a battle cry. She plunged back, whipping frosting into submission and wrestling layers into place, refusing to surrender to the culinary catastrophe.

For Thando, quitting was never an option. She embraced the challenges that life threw her way, viewing them as opportunities for personal growth. The quotes etched in her mind were a guiding light, reminding her that pain was fleeting, but the consequences of giving up were far-reaching.

*

In the weeks after the team-building retreat, Thando noticed the tension between her and Frans increasing. It became clear to her that there was only room for one strong personality in their office, all for the sake of the team's productivity. Frans and Thando's fake friendliness felt strained by an underlying rivalry. They greeted each other with quick nods instead of their usual friendly hellos, and even simple small talk seemed awkward and forced.

Thando felt frustrated. She wanted things to change. The usual routine no longer satisfied her, and she felt a strong urge to look for opportunities outside her continent. She craved a fresh narrative filled with new characters from diverse cultures and backgrounds, each with their unique way of life. She felt that exploring different cultures and backgrounds would broaden her perspective and understanding of the world. By immersing herself in the lives of characters from diverse backgrounds, she could learn about different traditions, values, and ways of thinking.

Beneath the surface, a more profound longing stirred within her heart. Her relationship with Harold also holds the key to her unspoken desire. She was becoming dissatisfied with the long-distance relationship and wanted more of him, craving his presence and warmth. She felt a stronger pull towards him as if some cosmic force was pushing their paths to come together.

Her decision to explore opportunities abroad wasn't just about her career. It was also about bridging the distance between her and Harold, weaving their lives together with love and shared dreams. Fate smiled her way, and she received an incredible offer from China Ltd., a prestigious global company based in Taiwan, a distant and vibrant land filled with life and energy. They saw her leadership potential and invited her to be the Vice President of New Business in the finance department. It was a chance to impact significantly a whole business unit and explore endless possibilities.

Thando's journey to her role in Taiwan was not a sudden leap; it was pushed by her deep desire to expand her horizons. Realizing her bitter situation with Frans, she consciously decided to stay out of his way. Instead, she focused her time and attention on seeking opportunities that would enable her growth and make a meaningful impact. She took on new challenges, honed her skills, and built a reputation as a dedicated and innovative leader among her peers.

When fate intervened in the form of an unexpected email from China Ltd., a prestigious global company with operations in Taiwan. She knew it was her chance to demonstrate leadership and show her ability to drive results in a dynamic business environment. Her passion for making a positive impact and her vision for the future of the company resonated with the hiring team,

The role they offered her was nothing short of a dream come true – the Vice President of New Business in the finance department!

Thando's heart brimmed with excitement and joy as she realized the magnitude of the opportunity. It was a chance to turn her aspirations into reality, a brave move towards her long-awaited success.

In the new role, she would be free to shape the future of an entire business unit, like an artist crafting a masterpiece from a blank canvas. Like a stone cast into still waters, her vision would create ripples of positive change and innovation, extending far beyond the boundaries of her imagination.

After years of hard work and perseverance, Thando's efforts were finally recognized and acknowledged. The sense of validation filled her with a warm glow of satisfaction. Thando felt an added layer of joy, knowing that the opportunity would bring her closer to Harold. With the new role in Taiwan, she could focus on her career and nurturing their relationship.

In her childhood, Thando had a cherished routine. She would walk a little over two kilometers to reach a forest that held a special kind of magic, not too far from her grandmother's house. The distance was perfect for her small feet, and it felt like she was stepping into a new world beyond her familiar surroundings. The forest was beautified with tall pine trees that embraced her with their soothing presence, providing a haven of solace and joy. Thando would immerse herself in books, getting lost in their captivating stories while enjoying the delightful sandwiches her grandmother lovingly prepared for her. These precious hours spent among the trees and pages of her books gave Thando a sense of freedom and peace away from the bustling noise of her cousins and friends.

The forest became her secret sanctuary, where she could escape and be one with nature. The soft whisper of leaves and the far-off cries of birds. Birds created a symphony that only added to the enchantment of the place. It was a world where her imagination could roam freely, and the worries of the outside world seemed to fade away. When Thando returned home, everyone was eager to hear about her adventures. She would happily share stories about the beautiful scent of the pine trees, the interesting things she discovered in the woods, and the fascinating people she met along the way. Her tales captivated everyone's imagination and left them wanting to hear more.

Thando was living her wish of traveling the world to different continents while working in a profession she loved. Her role required frequent travels to meet with customers all over the globe, allowing her to immerse herself in different cultures and connect with diverse individuals. Through her work, she formed meaningful friendships with many people who had become dear to her. Building connections came naturally to Thando, and making friends was something she excelled at without difficulty.

Just like in her relationships, Thando experienced challenges and complexities in her work relationships. She recognized that the dynamics within her work environment resembled those of an extended family. First, there was John, the master of blunt comments. He had a knack for speaking his mind, just like Thando's uncle, after a few drinks. You could always count on him to deliver a verbal punchline that left everyone stunned. Then, there was Rachel, the information queen. She knew everyone's business, like her dear aunt, her father's sister.

If there was some juicy gossip floating around, Rachel would be the first to spread it, making her the unofficial grapevine manager of the office. And not forgetting Andrew, the untouchable one. He somehow managed to receive undeserved praise and get away with things, just like Thando's spoiled cousin in her own family. It was as if Andre had a magical charm that shielded him from consequences.

With all the quirks and challenges, she understood the importance of maintaining professional boundaries, which required her to exercise patience and navigate these complexities in her work relationships.

Thando inherited a high-performing and independent team responsible for overseeing a region spanning over seventy countries, with a strong focus on the Asian market. The team's structure was unique, influenced by cross-cultural dynamics that made the reporting lines somewhat ambiguous. It took Thando over six months to fully grasp the organization's setup and identify the key decision-makers, but she received invaluable assistance from Su-Wei.

By the time Thando joined the company, Su-Wei, a celebrated member of the Taiwan management team, had already carved out a remarkable reputation for herself.

Her invaluable contributions were crucial in moving the business to unprecedented global success. With her striking Asian beauty and delicate features, Su-Wei possessed an undeniable allure that could easily grace the cover of prestigious magazines like Vogue. Her reserved nature belied the authority and clarity in her words, effortlessly commanding the respect of those around her.

The intriguing contrast between Su-Wei's composed poker face and the warmth emanating from her beaming smile truly captivated Thando's attention.

Thando and Su-Wei's professional relationship blossomed into a strong rapport rooted in mutual respect and a shared dedication to their work. They often collaborated on various projects, pooling their insights and expertise to achieve exceptional results. Recognizing Thando's struggle to establish camaraderie within her vertical teams, Su-Wei graciously offered her support and guidance.

As Thando faced the ongoing challenges of gaining trust and fostering unity among her team members, the difficulty of her situation seemed to intensify with each passing day. Her subordinates often questioned and challenged her, adding to more pressure on her shoulders. Not only had she inherited a struggling business unit that had failed to deliver positive results over the past three years, but she also had to navigate the treacherous waters of a toxic team culture.

*

New to her demanding role, she was utterly consumed by the immense pressures and challenges it presented. Unfortunately, during the overwhelming responsibilities, she unintentionally overlooked an important external meeting she had asked Su-Wei to arrange. Su-Wei arrived at Thando's office block just as the oversight regarding the meeting occurred.

It was a stroke of serendipity, for she had intended to remind Thando about the crucial engagement. With impeccable timing, Su-Wei stepped into Thando's office and immediately sensed the charged atmosphere as Thando engaged in a heated discussion with a business unit lead. The tension was palpable, and Su-Wei, ever perceptive, cleverly and respectfully excused Thando from the situation, understanding the need for a swift departure.

Seated together in the back of a taxi, en route to a customer meeting in the bustling central district of Taiwan—Xinyi—the rain poured relentlessly outside. Each raindrop pounded against the roof of the car, creating a rhythmic symphony. Inside the taxi, the air hung heavy, warm, and stagnant. It carried an unusual scent, a blend of a lemon-sprayed ashtray left to dry, adding to the surreal ambiance of the moment.

The taxi journeyed through the rain-soaked streets, and the sound of droplets on the rooftop was a backdrop to their conversation. Su-Wei leaned in, breaking the silence with her soft-spoken wisdom. "Office politics often arise from people who are uncomfortable or struggling with changes, whether it's with management or colleagues," she softly said, showing her understanding. "Remember, it's not personal."

"Of course," Thando replied, her gaze shifting from the uncomfortable stench to Su-Wei's reassuring presence. Though her voice exuded confidence, deep down, Thando hadn't fully considered the extent of the challenges that came with her role. Buried under a mountain of deadlines, she had found ways to navigate the situation, but the time felt different. She couldn't shake the feeling that it was more than a personal clash or misunderstanding.

Leaning forward, Thando took a moment to gather her thoughts before asking the question that had been lingering in her mind. "I've been meaning to ask you about Fong Hsu and his history within the organization," she inquired, her eyes focused on Su-Wei, searching for any hint of insight.

Fong Hsu, Thando's predecessor, successfully led the business unit for two years before abruptly moving on to head another part of the company in a different region. When Thando took over his role, she was assured that Fong would be available via email for the first month to provide a smooth transition. Thando tried to reach out to him for guidance and handover of pressing projects, but Fong had made himself conveniently unavailable, ignoring all her meeting requests.

Several factors contributed to Thando's suspicion surrounding Fong's sudden departure. Firstly, the way Fong abruptly left his position as the leader of the business unit raised eyebrows.

Even after successfully heading the team for two years, he seemed to vanish, transitioning to a new role in a different region within the company. Such a swift and unexpected departure left Thando wondering if there was a hidden reason behind it.

Secondly, Thando's assurances during her transition that Fong would be available via email for support and guidance turned out to be empty promises. When Thando attempted to reach out to him for classified information and the handover of projects, Fong conveniently made himself unavailable, ignoring all her meeting requests. The uncooperative behavior left Thando questioning whether Fong deliberately chose to evade her or if there was more to his avoidance.

Moreover, Thando's instincts told her that her hiring managers might have yet to provide the complete story behind Fong's departure. There was a lack of transparency regarding the circumstances surrounding his exit from the business unit. The discrepancy between what she was told and the reality of the situation stimulated her suspicion that there might be hidden information or undisclosed reasons behind Fong's sudden departure.

With her back straightened, Thando looked intently at Su-Wei, silently urging her to share any insights she might have about Fong Hsu's history and the hidden currents that swirled beneath the organization's surface.

The past three months had been exhausting for Thando, with mixed feedback from the teams and discrepancies between Fong's revenue forecasts and the actual results of the past three years. Despite her efforts to set up a meeting with Fong for clarification, he remained elusive and unavailable. Adding to her predicament, the other vertical business units seemed hesitant to grant her the authority to lead their projects. Thando felt trapped, torn between the conflicting forces at play.

Taking a deep breath, Su-Wei leaned in, her voice measured and tinged with a hint of caution. "Thando, I won't sugarcoat it. The insights I'm about to share may not be entirely factual. However, they might help you piece together the puzzle," she warned, understanding the pre-warning

Thando's eyes widened when Su-Wei shed light on the confusing situation surrounding Fong. It became clear that Fong's underperformance had not gone unnoticed by the executive team. Even though he couldn't deliver the expected results, Fong's father, as the board chairman, ensured his employment stayed secure.

Su-Wei continued, explaining that Fong's extensive network and ability to generate business for various ventures within the company were the reasons behind his relocation to oversee the emerging SpaceX business unit, with Vice President Louis providing supervision.

Listening attentively, Thando absorbed the information being shared. Su-Wei's voice took on a more reassuring tone as she added, "The way I see it, Thando, the rewards for successfully turning around the business unit could be substantial. it is crucial to acknowledge that the risks of failure are equally significant." Su-Wei emphasized her intention to present an accurate picture of the situation, aiming not to frighten Thando but to provide a realistic assessment from an external perspective.

On their taxi ride back to the office, Thando was quietly lost in thought, reflecting on Su-Wei's revelation. The seriousness of her situation weighed on her mind, presenting her with a complex juggling act. Not only did she have to skillfully handle the tricky dynamics of office politics, but she also had the responsibility of overseeing a struggling department in the company. The situation held an added layer of complexity- she was standing on a glass cliff.

VIII. Hanging on the Glass Cliff

Thando, a woman with her fair share of challenges and triumphs, took a moment to reflect on her career journey. A rush of emotions flooded her.

She remained proud and grateful for how far she had come through the ups and downs. Each obstacle she conquered left its mark, a testament to her resilience and determination. So did every setback and success she celebrated. They shaped her into the person she is today. She recognized her abilities as the driving force behind her accomplishments. She felt convinced.

Thando's decision to pursue the role of Vice President at China Ltd. wasn't made lightly. It was a choice born out of excitement and nerves, with a deep-seated belief in her capabilities. As she weighed the challenges ahead, she couldn't ignore the flicker of doubt that danced at the edges of her mind. Despite the doubts, a sense of determination burned bright within her, begging her to push forward.

Her past experiences had shaped her in ways she couldn't have anticipated. Each setback and obstacle had only strengthened her resolve to push forward. The scars she carried were more than physical reminders of past challenges; they were badges of resilience, proof that she had difficulties endured before and emerged more resilient.

Thando's way of navigating corporate politics was intriguing. It wasn't about playing by the rules. She had a knack for blending strategic thinking with natural charm. She knew that traditional tactics wouldn't cut it in the complex arena. Thando faced challenges in her role, which felt like being stuck on a "glass cliff."

Additionally, she faced hurdles due to her race. In a community dominated by Asian and Caucasian individuals, her unique skin color and mannerisms made her stand out. Simple gestures, like laughing in a high-pitched voice in public, drew attention to the contrast between her and the majority.

Thando observed Fong's former team. She discerned the intricate dynamics of their friendships. She also noticed the subtle currents of internal competition. During these observations, she also recognized the untapped potential within the group. Instead of immediately asserting her authority, Thando opted for a different approach. She prioritized building connections through friendly conversations and casual meetings. Thando fostered trust and cultivated positive relationships. It laid the groundwork for enhanced collaboration and mutual respect within the team.

Thando recognized the importance of forging connections with key board members. Leveraging her adept networking skills, she approached the task with a unique twist. She didn't stick to formal avenues. Instead, she embraced opportunities such as charity functions, community gatherings, and cultural festivals. Board members often attended these events. Thando had a chance to engage with them in a more relaxed setting. It fostered genuine connections and left a lasting impression.

Thando's strategy continued. She delved deeper, discovering these board members' personal interests and hobbies. Armed with this knowledge, she tailored her interaction, which helped create memorable experiences.

She quickly recognized that she needed more than showing her skills and achievements; she needed the right platform and audience. So, she initiated a series of interactive workshops and presentations within the company. These sessions highlighted her expertise and encouraged her colleagues' active participation, fostering collaboration and inclusivity.

*

Thando disregarded the office gossip, passive-aggressive behavior, and hallway chatter in the ensuing months. Her focus was on achieving tangible results, no matter the cost.

Thando faced the complexities of her race and grappled with being a woman in a patriarchal culture. Her presence and way of doing things made her team uncomfortable, evident through their uneasiness in her presence. Thando keenly sensed the discomfort surrounding her, further highlighting the uphill battle she faced.

The first transformation she pursued was in her wardrobe. She had a clear vision of assimilating into the corporate world. She instructed her assistant to buy business attire that reflected her ambition. The vibrant African prints, bold jewelry, and towering heels were gone. In their place were conservative blue and black business suits paired with modest kitten heels.

The chic, feminine dresses were gone too. They swapped them for knee-length options with higher necklines. Even Thando's casual Friday ensembles once featured hourglass jeans and colorful blouses. They underwent a metamorphosis to underscore her unwavering commitment to success. Thando signaled her readiness to navigate the new corporate landscape. She aimed to do so with finesse and determination.

Her team appreciated being at the forefront of these changes, and they warmed up to her approach as they witnessed her transformation.

Within the office, Thando made subtle adjustments to the teams, taking careful consideration to minimal disruption. She also hired a Technical Assistant to oversee financial and administrative transactions between business units that had previously been neglected. The delegation freed up considerable time for Thando and her team, allowing them to focus on forging stronger collaborations with key stakeholders and gaining support for significant projects. Thando paid no heed to the traditional ways of doing things; instead, she issued clear and precise instructions without seeking permission.

Through her multifaceted strategy, Thando's influence and reputation flourished within the organization. The tide began to turn, and it was impossible to ignore. Within six months of the business unit overhaul, the needle moved positively, even against challenging market conditions. Word spread throughout the company about Thando's exceptional achievements and her ability to accomplish the seemingly impossible.

Thando's impactful changes and the subsequent financial results were making waves in the industry press. Headlines were buzzing with discussions about her transformation and its positive effects.

Thando stood confidently among her coworkers, her presence commanding attention. Some marveled at her bold drive for success, hailing her as the potential hero of the company, akin to a modern-day Moses leading them to new heights. Alongside the praise were whispers of uncertainty, poisoned by conservative media outlets. One article cheered her on as a champion. While another hinted that her African background might cause problems, focusing on her race as a potential issue.

Thando's colleagues rallied behind her, yet she couldn't shake the pang of longing for official recognition she believed she deserved from the company. Their support was cherished but couldn't fill the void without acknowledging her significant contributions. The persistent lack of recognition began to chip away at Thando's morale and self-assurance. Despite her efforts to remain focused on her achievements, the feeling of being undervalued lingered. Day by day, she poured her heart into her work, but the mounting scrutiny from peers and superiors only exacerbated her frustration.

The constant barrage of criticism and skepticism took a toll on Thando's mental and emotional well-being. It chipped away at her self-assurance and fueled self-doubt about her abilities and contributions. Without the affirmation and validation she sought from the organization, Thando found maintaining her motivation and drive challenging. The lack of acknowledgment served as a constant reminder of her perceived inadequacies. She felt lonely and isolated.

"I know I can deliver exceptional results, but I'm not sure I can handle the relentless attack on my character and the lack of support from the board," Thando confided in Su-Wei, her trusted friend and confidante. Thando knew she needed to find a way to assert her worth and gain the recognition she deserved, but the path ahead seemed daunting.

Su-Wei nodded with empathy at the gravity of the situation. "I understand, Thando. Unfortunately, our society is not accustomed to seeing a black person, especially a black woman, in such a prominent leadership role. We're used to men, Caucasian men, taking charge and dictating our actions. But never has a person of color held a high-profile position like you. The situation could be jealousy and resistance from people like Fong and his supporters." Thando sighed, feeling the burden of being a black woman in a position that challenged the norms.

"I am proud of my identity as a black woman, and I cannot change that. Thando's voice quivered as she spoke, a hint of sadness in her tone. "If my race keeps overshadowing the good, I do," she said softly, a tear slipping down her cheek, " maybe the board needs to rethink their values."

*

Standing off-balance, Thando persevered, continuing to move forward. The immense pressure and relentless demands were starting to show. Those close to her noticed subtle changes in her appearance and behavior. It was as if a shadow had fallen over her once vibrant and radiant aura. It left behind a weariness that seemed to linger in her eyes. The dark circles under her eyes spoke volumes about the countless sleepless nights. She endured them while trying to meet her responsibilities.

Gone were the days of impeccable grooming and stylish attire she was once known for. Her appearance had become neglected. A mirror of the diminishing energy and self-care she had towards herself. A true reflection of the burden she carried on her shoulders and the toll it was taking on her well-being.

*

Harold noticed a decline in Thando's health and frequently visited Taiwan to check on her. He observed changes in her behavior, noticing that she had become withdrawn. Thando had started declining social invitations instead of social evenings out with friends. Thando started spending more time alone. A big change from her former self

Her once vibrant nature gave way to a more reserved and introverted demeanor. Conversations with her became shorter and lacked the usual engagement and enthusiasm. Fatigue had started to overshadow her ability to engage and connect with Harold.

Thando reluctantly listened to Harold's worries and gave her long-awaited vacation plans to her team. The timing couldn't have been worse. The vacation was set to begin immediately after she delivered the Q4 results to the board, a task grueling quarterly task.

When she stood before the attentive board members during that pivotal meeting, exhaustion and stress wore her down. Physically and mentally drained, Thando reached her breaking point. In a dramatic turn of events, her body succumbed to the mounting pressure, and she collapsed right in front of her colleagues.

A stunned silence washed over the room. The unexpected scene unfolded, punctuated by her colleagues' gasps of concern and murmurs of worry. Su-Wei sprang into action, rushing to Thando's side and calling for medical help. Witnessing Thando's strong and determined facade crumble in an instant was a jarring and unsettling moment for all.

*

"What am I doing here?" Thando woke up disoriented from her hospital bed. Startled by the nurse shining a bright light into her eyes. Her body weakened, and her mind filled with worry as she tried to lift her body, which felt like a large tree had fallen on her. "Don't kill yourself," Harold cautioned, hastily rushing to her side. He was still wearing his business suit, slightly rumpled from hastily leaving a meeting. Harold's red tie hung loosely around his neck. The once crisply tied knot slackened around his neck.

The medical staff, well-intentioned, struggled to make sense of her condition. They pointed to the flu as the culprit behind her symptoms—aches, fatigue, and a relentless cough.

Days turned into weeks as Thando's hospitalization extended. Language barriers posed a challenge. The nurses' gazes filled with intrigue and perplexity, as if her presence defied their expectations. Thando's diversity stood out in a homogenous population, adding an exciting twist to her time at the hospital.

Thando and Harold were grappling with translations, relying on gestures and her mobile phone to communicate her needs. The unfamiliarity of it all stirred her sense of vulnerability. Lying in her hospital bed, Thando felt like she was in a foreign land, far away from the familiar streets she called home. She noticed differences in culture. It became clear that being a black person brought about visible disparities in how people treated her. When she moved through the busy hospital corridors on good days. She experienced various reactions from other patients, from genuine interest and acceptance to subtle forms of discrimination and distrust.

Being diverse in a mostly homogeneous place added an interesting aspect to her hospital experience.

The language barrier presented an additional challenge for Thando. She struggled with translations and had to rely on gestures and fragmented conversations to communicate her needs. The unfamiliarity of it all made her vulnerable and resilient. She longed for a deeper connection to bridge the gap between her reality and the experience she had created up to that point.

Thando's journey in a foreign continent left a lasting impression during the three weeks she spent in that hospital in Taiwan.

Amid her challenges, she found unexpected moments of human connection and empathy. A gentle touch from a nurse or a smile exchanged with another patient comforted her. Thando understood that compassion and understanding could connect people across borders and cultural divides. These exchanges offered a profound truth that resonated with her- human compassion for herself and others.

Time seemed to slow down, and her heart filled with fortitude. The pressures of her responsibilities and what others expected of her seemed less important than her health. The outside world faded away at that moment, and her focus shifted to survival. She had a powerful realization of her value and the importance of being kind to herself. It was like a sudden thunderstorm that broke through the walls of self-doubt that had held her back for a long time.

She had a powerful realization of her value and the importance of being kind to herself. It was like a sudden thunderstorm that broke through the walls of self-doubt that had held her back for a long time. While her body's fragility reminded her of her mortality, it also ignited a strong spirit within her that refused to give up. With a determined gaze, Thando made a bold and freeing decision. She reached out and took hold of the resignation letter, which represented her release from the chains of a demanding job.

The impact of her sacrifice lingered around them. It meant leaving behind the familiar and embracing the uncertainty of what lay ahead. Though it may not have been a grand, dramatic moment, it was a significant choice for Thando. It was like a light bulb moment for her: she realized that her well-being mattered most, even if it meant walking away from a tough spot. She learned that there's nothing wrong with making a graceful exit. Taking the time to plan and consider her options made her departure appear like she was taking back control of her life.

She did not need to prove her worth.

Hey black child.
Be what you can do.
Learn what you must learn.
Do what you can do.
And tomorrow your nation
Will be what you want it to be.

IX. "EVOLVE OR DIE" DOUGLAS HOFSTADTER

Thando learned that even though it was customary to expect pushback, stepping onto a different path doesn't have to be a bumpy ride. Instead, it can serve as an empowering catalyst, moving her towards a fresh and promising phase in her life.

Six months into her sabbatical, she still felt a lingering tiredness, and her work situation hadn't changed. Restlessness crept in, and she began considering the idea of returning to work. She did not have a specific deadline, but she felt comfortable enough to dip her toes back into the business world. Her body was still recovering from the stress and shock she experienced during her time in Taiwan.

"I'm going to go for it. I know I can do it. I've been thinking about it for months now. I want to tell the stories that need telling," Thando shared with resolve. Harold looked at her with a blend of confusion and a childlike nervousness. "I want to start a company that helps black-owned businesses expand to global markets. "I've worked for big companies that preyed on third-world countries. Now, I want to use those skills to help and support black-owned businesses," Thando explained, assuring Harold of her sincerity.

"So, you want to be a reverse economic hitman and expose how the first world benefits from exploiting poverty and third-world resources?" Harold responded, trying to lighten the mood with a playful remark.

"Debt is the new form of slavery for most black-owned businesses in Africa. The way I see it, the global economic muscle enslaves more people than all the colonialists before us?" Thando remarked.

But as Thando's seriousness became plain, Harold enjoyed seeing Thando light up with purpose. After witnessing her physical and mental health deteriorate over the past two years, he felt relieved. But He secretly wished Thando would focus on their plans to start a family. He understood the importance of her calling, but he couldn't deny his desire for a different path.

"I am serious, Harold; I can't see myself doing anything else that would give me a grasp of purpose and fulfillment, "showing deep sincerity. "I understand your vision, and if anyone can make a difference, it's you," he said reassuringly, setting aside his unhappiness to lean in for a comforting kiss. Their tender kisses grew more passionate as they undressed, eventually finding themselves naked on the soft carpet of the living room. Thando's pleasure was palpable as she moaned with delight, holding onto Harold tightly, reluctant for the experience to end. Finally, reaching the peak of pleasure, her body exploded with satisfaction.

"Wow!" Harold exclaimed, taking a deep breath as he lay down, his back sweaty and marked from the encounter. Thando's invisible nail scratches on his back tingled in the warm air against the soft carpet. As if breathing new life into her, he whispered, "I missed you!"

*

Thando stood by the expansive window in her office, relishing the breathtaking view of the city below. Perched on the thirteenth floor of the Staten Island Business Center in New York, she had an unobstructed panorama of the bustling streets and towering skyscrapers. The sight filled her with empowerment and inspiration, igniting her drive for success.

Her office was meticulously designed to reflect her personal style and ambitious spirit. Hidden in a corner, it had handcrafted Haider Bioswing chairs and strong glass walls, letting lots of natural light brighten up the place. Each morning, she adorned her desk with fresh flowers, infusing the environment with a touch of nature and vitality.

One prominent feature of her office was displaying her company's name, Vice Capital, showcased in bold, golden letters on a bare wall. Below it, a hexagonal memo board held a collection of positive affirmations, reminding her of her vision and strength. Among those words of inspiration, a cherished photograph of her grandmother captured an appreciation of her heritage and wisdom. And the poem by Mr. Perkins added an air of intrigue, hinting at the ambitious path she was embarking on.

With a genuine smile, she cradled the warm cup of chai tea, relishing its comforting embrace. Her gaze fixed upon the towering skyscrapers that adorned the horizon, evoking a profound sense of awe and wonder within her. It felt like she had secured an exclusive front-row seat to a mesmerizing spectacle where dreams were meticulously built, each brick a testament to her goal.

At that moment, she paused for reflection, contemplating the essence of true success. It wasn't the grand spectacle she had imagined, with applause and public praise. Instead, it was a serene inner assurance, a quiet confidence resonating within her. She knew success wasn't about pursuing external validation but rather an internal state of being.

Her fantasies had once painted a vivid picture of grandeur and celebration. Picturing herself displaying her accomplishments to an audience of admirers, accompanied by the effervescence of champagne. But reality proved to be a far more profound truth – every achievement resulted from her endless dedication, resilience, and unwavering self-confidence.

The familiar sensation offered both comfort and disbelief. Thando had long visualized the moment of success, playing it over in her mind until it felt as though she was reliving a cherished memory, a déjà vu of victories savored a thousand times before. Success was no longer a distant dream she chased; it had woven itself into the very essence of her being, an intrinsic part of her identity. What was once a relentless pursuit had become her natural state, a quality radiating from the depths of her soul, as natural and essential as breathing.

Success was no longer an elusive goal she t pursued. It had become an integral part of her very being, interwoven into the fabric of her existence. The pursuit had transformed into a state of being. An intrinsic quality that emanated from deep within her soul. It showed how much she had grown, how tough she'd been, and how dedicated she was to her dreams.

Success! What an interesting concept! She giggled out loud.

*

Amsale interrupted her moment of deep reflection. She hurried into her office, conveying a sense of urgency with her gestures. "You have to come to see this; hurry up!" they exclaimed, waving their hand with urgency. During her pregnancy, Thando found moving difficult and was curious and slightly surprised. She got up from her chair, ensuring she didn't bump into the desk. She felt worried at the thought of the immobility, *"This baby is heavier than I thought. I can hardly imagine how much she weighs in the final months.'*

Thando waddled towards the door, taking cautious steps, when Amsale approached her. Thando and Sale licked instantly. Their friendship blossomed with time. Amsale's magnetic presence and warm demeanor made her approachable to everyone she met. Her genuine interest in people and their stories fostered an openness and trust in those around her. Amsale stayed grounded and humble by actively spearheading social causes and philanthropic efforts, dedicated to giving back to her community.

Amsale's leadership style was all about inclusivity and collaboration. She empowered her team to share ideas, fostering innovation within her company. Beyond her professional success, Amsale had a deep love for art, culture, and heritage. Her scarf designs often reflected Ethiopian culture, showing her passion for traditional craftsmanship.

As a great storyteller, Amsale inspired many with tales from her entrepreneurial journey. Her travels broadened her perspective and revealed her creativity, leaving a lasting impact on those she met.

To Thando, Amsale was more than a mentor; she symbolized hope. When Thando learned that Amsale lived in New York, she sought her guidance. Their conversations led to a partnership built on mutual respect and a shared vision.

Filled with anticipation, Amsale led Thando to a TV screen. To their surprise, they saw live press coverage featuring their fierce competitor, Hunter Ltd.

In a jaw-dropping reveal, Hunter Ltd. admitted to selling their clients' private financial details. The breach led to widespread financial ruin, with thousands losing their homes due to compromised bank accounts and fraudulent mortgages opened in their names. The news hit the industry hard. The clients affected ranged from hardworking low-income civilians in the U.S. to big-time corporations in Ghana. The shockwave rippled through the room, turning disbelief into outrage.

The drama intensified when the CEO shared a gut-wrenching update about a contract worker who, overwhelmed by despair, tragically took their own life. The revelation deepened the sense of betrayal and sorrow at the event.

What started as a typical corporate gathering quickly spiraled into a scene straight out of a movie. The final bombshell dropped when the CEO announced that Hunter Ltd. was shutting down for good. Tears were shed as the gravity of the CEO's words sank in, capturing the collective heartbreak of everyone involved. The scandal not only highlighted the devastating impact of data breaches but also underscored the need for stringent security measures and ethical business practices.

During the chaos, Thando was glued to the unfolding drama. The press corps relentlessly asked questions of the competitors, as though eager to expose their vulnerability to the world. It was like watching a real-life drama unfold on live television.

Rumors of their financial struggles had been circulating. But nobody, including Thando and her team, expected such a drastic turn of events. The industry was left reeling, embroiled in the biggest scandal to date. Heated debates erupted across various media platforms. Questioning foreign policies and the credibility of financial institutions.

Their competitor's actions exposed the very weaknesses she was set on challenging. Now, all that was left was to team up with the right institutions and put her proposed solution into action. Amsale was thrilled; another company's misstep had become their biggest opportunity.

Such was the nature of the game in the industry. In an environment where swift movements were crucial, adaptability was key, and change was constant. Each day brought its mix of blessings and curses. The gift of closing a lucrative deal could come with the risk of job losses. It was all part of the intricate dance within the industry. As the rest of her team engaged in animated discussions about the shocking turn of events. Thando waddled back to her office, downloading all sorts of emotions. Settling into her desk, she pulled out a piece of paper and a pen. With a determined hand, she wrote the words, "SUCCESS = EVOLUTION."

The sudden events took on a deeper significance for Thando, who had been savoring her recent accomplishments moments before. It served as a powerful symbol, confirming her thoughts about the essence of success. Success wasn't just about reaching a specific goal; it was an ongoing journey of growth and adaptation. The surge of joy from success is always followed by a persistent urge to keep evolving. The newfound perspective echoed a book she had encountered during her third year of university. A book by Charles Darwin's seminal work, "On the Origin of Species." In Darwin's insightful words, he described evolution as the process by which organisms change to adapt to their environment for survival, competition, and reproduction. Thando has always been fascinated by the idea that survival and success are intertwined.

She reflected on the concept of equating survival with success and how it aligned with her journey. Thando had poured her heart and soul into becoming the success she is today, but she realized that if she followed Thando, she thought about how her journey to success mirrored Darwin's theory. Pouring her heart into her career had brought her to that moment in time. But she then realized that sustaining and growing her success demanded ongoing dedication, echoing Darwin's ideas. In Darwin's insightful words, he described evolution as the process by which organisms are forced to change to adapt to their environment for survival. The drive that had brought her that far might not be enough for the future.

The next day, Thando walked into the office with a noticeable spring in her step. Unfazed by the heaviness of her growing belly,

Even in her second trimester, she felt a surge of energy, more like her vibrant self again. She was grateful for the absence of morning sickness and the ability to power through long days without needing a nap.

As she strolled through the open-plan area, she noticed the bustling scene before her. Her team of ten people was surrounded by desks piled high with inquiries from potential clients and small businesses. The office buzzed with activity as her team navigated the flood of requests.

Thando felt a swell of pride, witnessing the tangible results of their hard work.

*

Publications scrambled to secure an exclusive story, eager to be the first to deliver the shocking revelations unveiled by their competitor. The industry was submerged in a deep-rooted scandal, with an increasing number of clients coming forward, sharing their stories of being deceived into unethical contracts by influential Tier 1 banks.

As news of the scandal broke, publications vied for an exclusive story, striving to be the first to report on their competitor's shocking revelations. The industry became entangled in a scandal as more clients stepped forward, sharing their stories of being deceived into unethical contracts by prominent Tier 1 banks.

Finally arriving at her office, Thando prepared to settle in when her PA urgently signaled that she had an urgent call waiting in line.

"Hello, Mazibuko; how can I help you?" Thando answered, picking up the hold line and introducing herself by her last name. It was her preferred way of address. Only her close friends and family called her by her first name, and even then, they typically used the shortened version, calling her "T."

"Hello, Mrs. Mazibuko. This is Roger Harris from ABC News & Current Affairs Broadcasting. Thank you for taking my call," the voice on the other end greeted, not waiting for Thando to respond.

"First, before I jump into the reason for my call," he continued after clearing his throat, signaling the importance of his upcoming statement, "Congratulations on your company's recognition for its international outreach."

"Thank you. We are excited about the results," Thando replied.

"Yes... yes, I can imagine," Roger interjected, eager to move the conversation forward. "We would like to do a 30-minute feature on your business growth and include an opinion piece discussing the breach of ethical foreign policies by Hunter Ltd. Roger's words interrupted Thando's attempt to finish her sentence. "Okay," she replied, her voice hinting at reluctance. In her mind, suspicions about the intentions behind Roger's gesture raced. Could he set her up for another controversial discussion, exacerbating the scandal? She thought Roger might be planning an intriguing twist to the scandal. A company owned by Africans uses resources from developed countries to sell its people.

"Are you still there?" the voice on the other end of the call asked.
"

"Oh, yes, I'm still here. Thank you for the opportunity. Yes, I would be interested in participating. Please share the details with my PA, Lungi. You had a brief chat with her earlier, and she will assist in organizing everything," Thando responded, keeping her composure.

"Yes, of course. Thank you very much, Miss Masibukon," the person on the other end acknowledged.

"It's Mrs. Mazibuko," Thando corrected, emphasizing the "Mrs." and the crisp sound of the letter 'Z,' which could have been interpreted as rudeness. Enduring the mispronunciation of her last name was an annoyance she had to overlook, as she insisted on using her African maiden name instead of adopting Harold's last name.-Nicholas She knew adopting a Western name would make her business life easier and potentially open doors more quickly, but she was not one to be enticed by shortcuts.

"Oh, yes, please excuse me, Mrs. Mazibuko. I wanted to mention that we will air the interview as part of our highlight news of the week segment. We look forward to speaking with you next week. Have a great rest of the day," the voice on the call concluded.

The air reeked of scandal, enveloping the consultancy industry like a foul stench. Hunter Ltd.'s actions had stirred up a storm, attracting media sharks hungry for a juicy story. It was a feeding frenzy, with journalists circling, eager to pounce on any firm suspected of unethical behavior.

Thando noticed competitors expressing strong negative sentiments. One by one, associates positioned themselves to protect their business interests. As newspaper articles and news coverage continued to pile up, the pressure on Thando and Sale intensified. Each piece brought them closer to a critical juncture, where they would have to step forward and seize the perfect moment to speak up.

*

Thando could not shake off the grip of doubt that had firmly taken hold of her heart. Night after night, she tossed and turned, desperately searching for a comfortable position. The size of her growing belly only added to her discomfort, and her mind raced tirelessly, denying her a good night's rest. Anxiety consumed her, and she toyed with the idea of suggesting to Sale that they switch places for the upcoming interview, hoping to shield herself from the potential pitfalls that awaited her. Sale's reminder echoed in her mind, reminding her of the challenging journey she had embarked on to reach that crucial moment. Years of dedication and hard work had brought her here, and she had to summon the courage to step forward and claim her rightful place. Thando acknowledged the truth in Sale's words, even if they did little to alleviate her lingering fears.

*

On interview day, she was joined by Lungi, her ever-enthusiastic Personal Assistant. Lungis excitement was infectious. She couldn't contain her joy at the thought of visiting the prestigious ABC studios.

Arriving at the broadcasting studio thirty minutes early, Thando took the opportunity to relax, grab a bite to eat, and gather her thoughts. As the interview approached, a shiver of anticipation ran down her spine, reminding her of the moment's importance. Her mind buzzed with thoughts. Sifting through words and phrases in search of the perfect combination to tackle any challenges.

The phrases she had practiced repeatedly seemed to evade her at the crucial moment, a common sensation in live interviews. But this time felt different. Thando was aware of the scrutiny she was under, knowing that every word she uttered would be dissected and used against her. The stakes felt higher than ever, hanging heavy in the air, intensifying the tension in the room.

As Thando settled into her chair and glanced past Roger into the live camera, something remarkable occurred. The fear and anxiety that had plagued her before the interview dissolved, replaced by an intense laser focus. At that moment, she experienced a surge of adrenaline coursing through her veins, a sensation she had never felt before. Her entire perspective shifted. She realized that the media was not out to attack her; rather, they were genuinely curious about who she was and what she had to offer. Deep down, she had known that all along, but her fears and anxieties had clouded her judgment. Calm emotions washed over her mind, and words flowed eloquently from her lips.

"Do you have any parting shots for our viewers?" Roger inquired, his warm look signaling that the interview was ending positively.

"Yes, Roger," Thando responded confidently. We take our work seriously and are incredibly proud of the achievements we've made in the past year. We are dedicated to helping businesses expand to all corners of the world, where they can continue to thrive and generate value."

"The results speak for themselves," Roger interjected.

"Indeed, and we remain open to collaborations with individuals who share our enthusiasm and vision for growth," Thando added.

"Thank you. That was Thando Mazibuko, founder and CEO of Vice Capital, a company dedicated to enforcing ethical policies to drive client growth," Roger concluded.

"Thank you, Roger," Thando replied, rising from her seat to shake Roger's hand and remove her microphone. She noticed Lungi approaching with a panicked expression.

Thando came down from the stage, her heart pounding with worry as she approached Lungi. "What's happened, Lungi?" she inquired, sensing the distress in her colleague's expression. Lungi's voice trembled as she relayed the news, her words heavy with sorrow. "It's your grandmother... She had a fall at home, and they couldn't get her to the hospital in time. I'm so sorry, Thando. She's gone. At that moment, the world around Thando seemed to blur, and a fog of disbelief enveloped her.

*

Thando and Harold sat silently at the dinner table, their hearts heavy from the devastating news that Lungi had delivered. Harold's warm meal sat untouched as the dimmed lights cast a soft glow on the room. They pulled the curtains back, allowing the gentle moonlight to filter in, creating a serene atmosphere. As they drove home, Thando stayed quiet, lost in her thoughts. They drove through the streets until they reached Thando's house. Harold was waiting for her there.

"Please, my love, you have to eat something," Harold softly urged, his voice filled with genuine concern.

"I can't bring myself to eat. I still cannot believe it," Thando replied, her voice filled with disbelief and sorrow as she stared blankly at her plate. It seemed futile to even consider lifting her fork to her mouth.

"I understand. Maybe there's something else I can find for you. You need to keep your energy up, especially for the baby," Harold suggested, his voice filled with empathy and understanding.

"I was supposed to be on a flight to KZN right now. I do not know... I should have been there with her, Harold. Instead, I am here, preparing for a TV interview. She was always there for me, and in her moment of pain, I was not there for her," Thando confided, tears welling up in her eyes.

"You couldn't have known, my love. Your grandmother was healthy, even at her age. There was no way to anticipate this," Harold consoled, reaching out to hold Thando's hand, offering comfort in his touch.

"It just doesn't make any sense. We were supposed to celebrate Gogo's 80th birthday next month. What do we do now?" Thando sighed, her voice heavy with confusion and sadness. The shock of the news had clouded her reasoning, leaving her emotions in disarray. The grief of her grandmother's loss overwhelmed her, coupled with the burden of guilt.

"We'll find a way, Thando. Take a moment to relax. Try to eat something, even if it is just a little. I've already messaged Lungi to plan our trip for tomorrow morning. I will also inform your cousin

Dumisa that we're coming. For now, focus on caring for yourself and gathering strength for you and the baby. I will start packing our bags," Harold reassured, rising from his seat and making his way to their bedroom to begin the preparations for their journey to Thando's grandmother's village, where she would be laid to rest.

Alone at the dinner table, Thando was left to wrestle with her thoughts. She silently replayed the different scenarios that could have led to her grandmother's untimely passing, tears streaming down her cheeks, mingling with the untouched food before her. As she gazed at her dinner, she felt a gentle flutter in her stomach. '*I must be really hungry,*' she thought, reaching for her fork. But before she could take a bite, the flutter transformed into a more distinct nudge, a reminder of the life growing within her.

"Harold... come quickly!" she called out, her voice filled with emotions of excitement.

"What is it?" Harold hurried to Thando's side, tripping over a forgotten bag at the entrance in his eagerness. "Are you all right? Is the baby okay? Can you breathe?" His worry was evident as he frantically voiced his concerns.

Thando placed Harold's hand on her belly, a warm smile spreading across her face. "Just wait for it," she said softly, tears streaming down her cheeks.

"He's moving..." Harold exclaimed with joy, his voice filled with childlike laughter. He felt the gentle kicks beneath his hand. "He moved again. With kicks like those, it is our boy," he declared, his voice resonating with pride and excitement, affirming his role as a father.

"It could be a girl," Thando chuckled, a hint of humor returning to her voice. "My grandmother was convinced it was a girl. She was right about you, so maybe she's right about the baby's gender, too."

At that moment, amid their shared laughter and joy, they found solace in life's bittersweet contrast.

*

The long and uncomfortable flight to KwaZulu Natal had exhausted Thando, swaying her feet and causing overall discomfort. Even though they had business-class seats, she could not find a comfortable position and felt restless. She was tired, filled with emotions, and desperately craving a comforting home-cooked meal.

When the plane landed at King Shaka International Airport, Thando and Harold were tired and emotionally vulnerable. Her cousin Nhlanhla warmly embraced them, his eyes filled with overwhelming emotions. They held onto each other tightly, shedding tears of joy as they reunited after more than four years, reigniting the unbreakable bond they had formed while growing up together.

While many of their childhood friends had left their hometown to pursue dreams in the city, Nhlanhla had chosen a different path. He found happiness in the simple life in Dukuza, living with his mother and later building a family with his wife and two children. He had no interest in material possessions or fancy titles, and Thando admired his contentment. In contrast, Thando felt weighed down by her ambitions, sometimes threatening her sanity and pushing her to her limits.

As the car hummed along the road, Thando and Nhlanhla dove into their shared history. Their conversation carried out in the comforting rhythms of Zulu, swept them through a twister of memories. They swapped family updates, reminisced about childhood antics, and revisited the simpler times of their youth.

In the back seat, Harold watched their lively exchange with a mix of admiration and nostalgia. Though he couldn't understand their words, he felt the closeness between the cousins. Despite the sadness of their trip, their laughter filled the car, casting a warm glow on the heavy circumstances. It cast a warm glow on the heavy circumstances we were facing.

In that moment, Harold found solace in the enduring strength of family ties, a reminder that love knows no language barriers.

The funeral reception, held in honor of Thando's grandmother, was a grand affair that suited the regal presence her grandmother had in their lives. The small village, once quiet and peaceful, transformed overnight into a bustling town as people from all over came to pay their respects out of love for her. Family, friends, and colleagues traveled from near and far to bid their final farewells to Gogo, as she was affectionately called.

On the day of Gogo's final celebration, the local church over-flowed with family and grandchildren. Usually intimate and cozy, only they could find space inside. The rest of the community gathered outside under tents, watching the proceedings on large monitors.

There was a tangible sense of immense love and admiration for Gogo. Her impact on the lives of those around her was undeniable, as shown by the thousands who came to pay their respects. Gogo was not particularly religious. She always emphasized the power of love. She shared how her belief in God had guided her journey. She touched many lives, leaving a lasting impact with her kindness and belief.

For Thando, it brought immense comfort to hear from various people about how much her grandmother cherished life, family, and the community. The family shared stories of Gogo's simple, joy-filled existence, highlighting how little she needed to find happiness— a phone call from her grandkids, her favorite gummy bear sweets from the city, or an impromptu visit from her children or neighbors meant the world to her. Above all, her family's well-being was her top priority, and she took a genuine interest in every aspect of their lives. She lived to improve their lives and never missed an opportunity to express her pride in all of them.

Thando herself was a blend of emotions. Between pregnancy hormones, exhaustion, and the profound sadness from the loss, it was a daily struggle to hold back tears. Harold remained steadfast, fearing the stress could cause premature labor or a miscarriage. He had concerns about Thando's well-being. Needing support, he confided in Thando's mother. Together, they agreed it would be best for Thando and Harold to leave immediately after the funeral. When Harold broached the topic with Thando, she didn't object. She was still dealing with her heartache, and her emotions detached from her current reality.

Their trusted assistant, Lungi, arranged their return flights. Thando's mother bid farewell to the rest of the family and drove them to the airport. Their departure was filled with mixed emotions. The loss of Gogo weighed on their hearts, but even with the sadness, there was a glimmer of hope for a new chapter in Thando and Harold's lives. With a sense of anticipation, they set on their journey back home.

*

"It feels like I'm trapped in a nightmare," Thando whispered, her voice filled with sadness and disbelief.

"I get it," Harold replied softly, his eyes showing concern. He carefully arranged extra pillows behind her back and reclined her seat to make her more comfortable before take-off. "Once they give us the okay, I'll ask for more blankets. I'm glad we managed to grab the last seats on this packed flight."

Thando nodded, tears welling up in her eyes. "This week has been so tough," she said quietly, her voice trembling. She reached out to Harold's hand, finding comfort in his warm touch. "But do you think everything will be alright?" she asked, her voice tinged with vulnerability.

Harold gently squeezed her hand, his love and support shining through. "Yes, my love," he whispered, his voice filled with fortitude. "We'll face whatever comes our way together."

Thando closed her eyes, hoping to escape the pain and confusion that had taken hold of her. As the plane soared into the sky, she allowed herself to drift off to sleep, finding solace in the serenity of slumber for the remainder of their journey back to New York.

At the peak of her career success, Thando faced the toughest emotional challenge ever. The overwhelming setback shook her to her very core. The grief she carried felt like an immense weight, relentlessly pressing down on her and threatening to crush her spirit. The recognition and praise she had once cherished seemed insignificant compared to the deep sorrow that consumed her. It was a heart-wrenching moment of vulnerability, where the clear boundaries between her personal and professional achievements blurred, leaving her in a fog of confusion and pain. The experience pierced her soul and revealed the intense and complex nature of human emotions.

*

"I have to go back there. My heart and soul belong there," Thando whispered, her voice trembling with sorrow. It had been a few weeks since her grandmother passed away, and her absence hung heavy on Thando's shoulders.

Harold, Thando's partner, could see the melancholy that enveloped her. He understood the turmoil she was experiencing and wanted to offer support, but he also knew the importance of careful decision-making during emotionally charged times.

As he gently voiced his concerns about her business and how she would explain her sudden departure to her team, furrowing his brows in worry, Thando felt overwhelmed. Her anxiety surged, and she feared it might push her into early labor.

"Don't add to my anxiety, please," she pleaded, her voice laced with exhaustion. She knew Harold meant well, but the pressure of the situation was already taking its toll on her well-being.

Harold took a deep breath, understanding her fragile state. He had been trying to comprehend her thought process, aware that their baby was due next month, and Thando needed all the strength she could muster for their child's arrival.

Sensing escalating stress, Thando's frustration erupted. Slamming her mug onto the kitchen counter, she snapped, "Stop calling her him!" Her words bring life to the emotional turmoil within her.

Sensing the moment's intensity, Harold reached out to calm her, his voice gentle and firm. "Please, my love, let's find peace during these challenging times. We need to focus on the present and the well-being of our baby. We can visit your family once our child is born."

Thando shook her head, tears streaming down her face. "You don't understand, Harold. Gogo was a beacon of selflessness, dedicating her life to volunteering and empowering our community. She gave tirelessly without expecting recognition. But here I am, living in the comfort of the first world, while my people struggle to progress."

Her voice trembled as she continued, "It's my responsibility to honor her legacy, to shine a light on all she stood for. I cannot let her efforts fade away in the shadows. I need to go back."

*

Amsale understood Thando. Their connection went beyond just work; they had a strong bond like sisters. Amsale could relate to Thando's emptiness because she had also lost her mother—a dedicated nurse who served others but never got to enjoy the rewards.

Thando trusted Amsale with her heartfelt conversations about Harold and her longing to return to Africa. Amsale listened attentively, understanding Thando's desire to find a place she could call home. They sat together, aware of the burden of their shared dreams and ambitions. Amsale sipped her green tea, which had since gone cold. After closing another major deal, they faced a challenge: limited resources and capacity. Thando carefully considered the situation and said, "I think we should expand and diversify our partnerships to handle all of them. It may seem risky, but we have to take the chance." Thando looked at Amsale, who nodded in agreement, fully aware of the importance of their decision. They believed they had no choice but to embrace every business opportunity, learning and growing as they went along to provide exceptional service.

For Thando, making the most of every opportunity was crucial. She believed in second chances but was determined not to rely on them. She knew that opportunities for girls like her, from her background, were rare and usually taken by those with connections. So, she decided to seize each opportunity she had, driven by her strong will to succeed against all odds.

"I agree with you. It will be a lot of work, but we can do it," Thando affirmed, her voice resonating with resolve as she aligned herself with Sale. Her words dispelled any doubt and left no room for further discussion. "What was I asking? Was it about your desire to move back home?"

Thando's gaze momentarily dropped to her stomach. Her mind was racing with conflicting thoughts, but deep within her, an undeniable longing tugged at her heartstrings. "I'm not sure what to do, Sale. I just know that it is something my soul wants to do. I have a strong urge to go back, but..."

Sale interrupted gently, sensing Thando's hesitation. She walked towards the window, captivated by the breathtaking sight of the vibrant orange skyline that had just painted the city. A profound sense of awe washed over her as she realized the beauty of following one's instincts. At that moment, she knew she had to share her own story. "I believe in signs and omens. I would never have left Ethiopia alive if I hadn't followed mine."

Pulling out her phone, Sale captured a picture of the awe-inspiring skyline before turning to face Thando. Her voice held a perfect blend of conviction and compassion. "Follow your heart, Thando. It will never lead you astray. Sometimes, the path ahead may seem uncertain, but when you listen to your soul's whispers, you find the courage to embrace the unknown."

Thando's eyes welled up when the drag of her decision settled in her mind. "I wish my grandmother was still alive to give me advice. How ironic is that?"

"Maybe she is," Sale responded softly, her gaze fixed on her growing belly, subtly emphasizing her statement. The room seemed to fill with an ethereal presence as if the spirits of their loved ones were watching over them. Amsale's love and support radiated from her, enveloping Thando in a warm embrace of reassurance. In that moment, Thando felt an inexplicable calmness wash over her, erasing her fears and uncertainties. She knew she had found a haven in the storm where she could nurture her dreams and embrace her calling.

Tears streamed down Thando's face as she nodded, her heart swelling with gratitude for her friend's support. In that shared moment, they forged an unbreakable bond, bound not just by friendship but by the profound journey they were about to embark on together. As they gazed out at the breathtaking skyline, they knew that no matter what challenges lay ahead, they had each other and the strength of their dreams to guide them.

*

The conference room door swung open, revealing the CEO of Sazi Ltd, who greeted Thando in a deep, authoritative voice, saying, "Welcome." Thando entered the room and confidently made her way towards an unoccupied chair at the head of the table, passing the nine executives, seven men, and two women, all impeccably dressed in professional attire. As she walked, Thando caught a pleasant blend of rose and musk fragrances wafting through the air. Being heavily pregnant, she had chosen to wear all black to discreetly conceal her belly despite its size.

Lungi, aware of the moment's significance, walked beside Thando, carefully carrying the materials for the presentation. The significance of the Vice Capital opportunity was evident in Lungi's eyes, betraying a hint of nervousness. In the preceding weeks, she had diligently sent out meeting invitations to the top five partner investors, both existing and potential clients, pitching a project that Vice Capital believed held immense potential. Coordinating such an exclusive gathering was no small feat. Still, to Thando and Amsales' astonishment, all ten CEOs had agreed to attend on the condition that the meeting be held offsite at one of their client's prestigious golf resorts, a forty-five-minute drive from the city.

Understanding the situation's urgency, Thando wasted no time engaging in small talk. She opened the meeting by expressing gratitude to the CEO of Sazi for providing exceptional facilities. Lungi efficiently moved around the table, distributing the meticulously prepared ten-page folder that had consumed their efforts for weeks. Once the last folder was placed, Lungi turned towards

Thando, who nodded, indicating that she should proceed to the next item on the agenda. All eyes in the room followed Lungi as she approached the door. Two strong individuals stood at the entrance, expertly maneuvering a massive table, towering twenty feet high and twenty-five feet wide, covered with a pristine Caucasian cloth, and positioning it precisely in the center of the room.

Thando politely thanked the individuals as they left the room. She walked forward confidently and stood before the table, summoning all her strength to remove the heavy Caucasian cloth. As the cloth fell, revealing the impressive display beneath, she commanded the attention of everyone present. "Ladies and gentlemen, I am proud to present to you Theku City—the city of the future." Thando's voice resonated with conviction, capturing the undivided attention of each person in the room. "This is a remarkable opportunity to invest in the forefront of sustainable living in one of KwaZulu Natal's most awe-inspiring cities."

*

The conference room door swung open, and Thando was greeted by the CEO of Sazi Ltd in a deep, authoritative voice, saying, "Welcome." With grace, she navigated her way to an unoccupied chair at the head of the table, passing the seated executives—seven men and two women—all impeccably dressed in formal business attire. As she entered, a subtle and pleasant fragrance of rose and musk permeated the air. Despite trying to conceal it, Thando was conscious of her prominent baby bump, elegantly concealed beneath an all-black ensemble.

Walking beside Thando was Lungi, who nervously carried all the materials for their critical presentation. Lungi understood the immense significance of the moment for Vice Capital, which was evident in the anxiety flickering in her eyes. In the weeks leading up to that day, she had diligently sent meeting requests to the top five partner investors—both existing and potential clients—pitching a project that Vice Capital believed presented a remarkable opportunity. Organizing such an exclusive gathering proved to be a significant undertaking. Thando and Amsales' surprise, all ten CEOs agreed to meet on the condition that the meeting took place offsite at a prestigious golf resort belonging to one of their clients, a forty-five-minute drive outside the city.

Aware of the time pressure, Thando skipped the pleasantries and entered the meeting. She started by thanking the CEO of Sazi for the venue. Lungi moved around the table, handing out the ten-page folder they had prepared for weeks. After placing the last folder, Lungi glanced at Thando, who nodded, indicating to move on to the next agenda item. All eyes followed Lungi as she walked towards the door. At the entrance, two individuals maneuvered a massive table. It was twenty feet high and twenty-five feet wide. With precision, they positioned it in the center of the room, covering it with a clean cloth.

As the gentlemen exited, Thando graciously thanked her and took her place before the table. Summing up her strength, she removed the heavy cloth, unveiling what lay beneath. Speaking with conviction and commanding presence, she proclaimed, "Ladies and gentlemen, I present to you Theku City—the city of the future." Thando's words demanded the full attention of everyone in the room.

"This represents an exceptional opportunity to invest in the future of green living, situated in one of KwaZulu Natal's most beautiful cities. Our project aims to establish a lifestyle of health and well-being through holistic practices powered by self-sustainable methods and cutting-edge technologies. Your investment and support will breathe life into this vision."

While "Theku" did not hold immediate significance to outsiders, it carried deep meaning for Thando and her family. It was a nod to the principles of holistic living that Thando's grandmother cherished and worked to uphold in Dukuza. The project would be a fitting testament to her grandmother's legacy. It was a heartfelt tribute to her grandmother's enduring legacy and the values she instilled in them.

The room fell silent as everyone absorbed the impact of Thando's words and the immense opportunity that awaited them.

Lungi stood at the back of the room. Her gaze swept over the crowd, noting the furrowed brows and puzzled expressions on everyone's faces. She determined to dissolve the thick cloak of unease around the situation. She took a decisive step forward and activated the video embedded in the 3D model of the city, triggering a cascade of vibrant visuals. An immersive soundtrack accompanied the visuals. The room bathed in a soft glow as the lights dimmed, and the video began unfolding before their eyes. It was a tapestry of pure bliss: birds soared overhead, their melodic chirps filling the air with a symphony of nature's song.

Laughter echoed as families frolicked in verdant parks. Wildlife sanctuaries buzzed with the lively chatter of diverse creatures going about their day. But the scene-stealer was the sight of children playing by a cascading waterfall. Their laughter mingled with the gentle rush of water as they splashed and danced with unrestrained joy. It was a tableau of serenity and vitality, a glimpse into an ideal world where humanity and nature coexisted in perfect harmony. At that moment, Lungi's bold move had transformed the atmosphere. It invited everyone to immerse themselves in the idyllic vision of life. It was a reminder that amidst the chaos of modern existence, there was still beauty to be found. Embracing a holistic approach to living, where the rhythms of nature and the joys of community were celebrated with open arms.

The short movie failed to interrupt the silence in the room. Thando sensed that the concept diverged greatly from the sky-scraper projects and high-yield investments she had pitched before, failing to capture their interest as she had hoped. The executives remained unconvinced by the "kumbaya" project.

Finally, an executive spoke up, voicing the question that lingered in everyone's mind: "What will be our return on this project? I'm not sure what you're asking of us."

Thando swept her gaze across the room, her heart pounding and the air thickened with anticipation. Every eye fixed on her, the silence swelling into a palpable tension that hung heavy in the atmosphere. Despite her preparation, a flow of nerves washed over her. It made her words clumsy and heavy in her mouth. She could sense the restlessness of her audience. Their expectations weighed on her like a ton of bricks.

With each passing moment, Thando's confidence wavered. Should she stick to her script and hope for the best, or dare to change tactics mid-speech? Pressure mounted as she weighed her options. The room seemed to shrink around her as if closing in on her dilemma.

In that split second of uncertainty, Thando's mind raced with possibilities. It was time to ditch the plan and speak from the heart, to connect with her audience on a more personal level. The fear of deviating from the script held her back. Expectations pressed down on her like a heavy burden.

Despite the temptation to shake things up, Thando stuck with her original plan. She pushed through the nerves with determination. It was a risk, one she was willing to take in pursuit of success.

"Thank you for the question, Mr. Steyn," Thando replied, making a deliberate effort to establish eye contact with each executive in the room. She understood that her future was at stake, and their investment was the key to revitalizing Dukuza and honoring her grandmother's legacy.

"People are already creating their communities. How is this venture different?" Jody Caucasian, representing the former Hunter Ltd (now acquired by Fox & Co.), asked.

"People are building DIY communities without the expertise of engineers and architects," Thando explained. "I'm not here to judge whether it's right or wrong, but what I'm suggesting is that THIS!" she pointed emphatically at the model of the city, "could be the solution they don't realize they need. The current community initiatives could lead to environmental disasters in the future. The people involved lack expertise in areas like global warming and sustainable energy. We can provide an ecosystem that ensures these communities are safe, sustainable, and poised for future success, with the right education and infrastructure." Thando paused, taking a deep breath.

"While we may not be construction experts, each of you in this room has been selected because of your expertise in recognizing potential and investing in it," Thando continued. "It's not just about the money; it's about unlocking possibilities that money can create!" She took another deep breath and carefully lowered herself into the nearest chair, sensing the pressure on her feet and the weight of her growing baby.

"Are you okay?" Jody asked, concerned by Thando's expression of pain. Lungi rushed to her side and offered a glass of water.

"Should we call a doctor? Someone, please call a doctor!" Mr. Steyn panicked, noticing water trickling down from her chair.

"There's no time!" Lungi exclaimed with urgency, supporting Thando. "I need help to get her to the car." Lungi and Mr. Steyn joined forces, placing Thando in the back seat. Lungi sat beside her as Jody maneuvered through the congested traffic, racing towards the hospital.

They had been anticipating the moment and prepared for it. Lungi followed the steps like a devoted soldier:

1. "Send Harold the code word: NOW!"
2. "Text or call her doctor."
3. "Retrieve her hospital bag from the trunk." Thando had carried it everywhere during her third trimester.
4. "Keep Thando calm."
5. "Discourage her from pushing."

Thando entered the delivery room, Lungis's face displaying excitement and urgency. The medical team sprang into action, their movements precise and well-coordinated. Machines beeped, filling the room, while hushed conversations added to the growing tension. Other mothers in labor could be heard crying in the center of it all, intensifying the emotional depth of the moment.

"Wh-When did you get here?" Thando gasped, eyes wide, and her voice filled with surprise as she noticed Harold standing beside the nurse dressed in scrubs. Harold had a knack for being there when it mattered most. Just like when Thando went through a tough time, he was by her side as she gave birth to their baby. His presence made her feel safe and at ease, like a familiar and steady support amid all the chaos.

"I wouldn't miss the birth of our first child for anything," he whispered, his voice filled with love. Leaning over, he pressed a gentle kiss on her forehead, his touch expressing a mixture of love and reassurance. With a firm grip, he held her hand tightly against his chest.

*

Thando's heart swelled with gratitude and affection as she looked into Harold's eyes. At that moment, she felt an unbreakable bond, a shared commitment to the new chapter of their lives. Thando went through her labor, and the passing hours seemed to merge. Time felt both quick and never-ending as she dealt with the ups and downs of pain, relying on her inner strength. The room echoed with the constant support and encouragement from the medical team, urging her to keep going and to push harder.

Contrary to what she had read in birth magazines, the baby surprised Thando by arriving earlier than she expected. Overwhelmed with various emotions, Thando held her newborn baby girl while the nurses positioned them for a family photo. In that special moment, Thando's heart overflowed with happiness and tiredness.

Soon after, the medical team took the baby and Harold away, disappearing down the hospital corridor. Harold, still caught up in the intense emotions of witnessing the birth, seemed dazed as he quickly said goodbye to Thando. Left alone in the quietness of her room, Thando's body continued to shake from the remaining adrenaline, and the effects of the medication gradually pulled her into a deep and peaceful sleep.

The next morning, as Thando woke up, the soft morning light filled the room with a gentle glow. Amsale, a close friend and confidante, stood at the foot of Thando's bed, holding a beautiful bouquet. Unable to contain her excitement, Amsale exclaimed, "Congratulations on the birth of your baby!"

Still groggy from sleep, Thando found Amsale's voice surprisingly loud. Her ears, sensitive to even the smallest sounds, made everything echo louder than usual. Trying to understand it,

Thando responded, "Why are you shouting? And remember, it is only one baby. We have not decided on a name because Harold was convinced it would be a boy. Right now, we're thinking of Zhara Wright."

Amsale smiled warmly and gently placed the bouquet on the table beside the bed. With a smooth movement, she pulled back the curtains, allowing the morning sunlight to flood the room. Amsale continued, "In that case, it's Zhara and Theku City. Yesterday, Mr. Steyn confirmed that you received eight 'yes' votes from the CEOs. It is a great achievement! Congratulations!"

Taken aback by the unexpected news, Thando tried to sit up and felt a sharp pain in her back. She winced and settled back onto the soft pillows, feeling happiness and apprehension about what the future held.

Amsale hurried to Thando's side, saying, "Take it easy, Tiger." She helped Thando find a comfortable position and assured her, "I'm not joking. You, Harold, and little Zhara will go to KZN when you're ready." Amsale paused, her eyes shining with excitement, before adding, "But for now, let's focus on Zhara. I will ask Lungi to collect the necessary signatures and finalize the investment plans. She will send the required documents to your home. Once you're better, we can arrange a meeting with the committee to make everything official."

The impact of these new developments rested heavily on Thando. Excitement and gratitude surged within her heart. Holding Zhara in her arms, her heart swelled with love and hope, ready to navigate the incredible path of motherhood and embrace all the blessings and challenges it would bring.

*

Lungi had arranged for a night nurse for the first four days, allowing Thando to finally get a few nights of uninterrupted sleep.

After a week of settling back into the routine at home with the baby, Thando regained her usual sense of self.

When the night nurse left and shut the door, the noise startled Thando and the baby, causing Thando to go to the baby's room to comfort her. It was the first time they were alone together since the baby was born. Thando looked at her baby's face with amazement, realizing she had helped create this beautiful life. The day the baby was born went by so quickly that Thando didn't have a chance to really see her face or fully appreciate what had happened. Now, as she nursed her baby in the peacefulness of the room, Thando closed her eyes and focused on her breath, listening to the precious sounds her baby made. It was a moment of newness and wonder for Thando, realizing that she had almost let it pass her by without giving herself a chance to fully absorb and cherish the experience.

As Zhara outgrew her tiny clothes, it reminded Thando that she needed to return to work and make progress on Project Theku. Each day, she contemplated different scenarios, debating when she should start.

"Perfect conditions don't exist. If I had waited for everything to be perfect, I would not have come this far in my career," Thando expressed, her desire to overcome evident.

"I understand that; maybe we can wait until Zhara is a bit older," Harold replied.

"She'll be older tomorrow, Harold. What does 'older' even mean? There will never be perfect conditions. Instead, let us view it in this way: if we start when conditions are at their worst, things can only get better from there!" Thando looked at Harold thoughtfully, realizing she was making another pitch to seek his support, only this time for love; it would be for love.

"I may never fully grasp your reasoning since you have investors waiting for this project to launch; it seems our options are limited," Harold admitted, looking away to conceal his disappointment.

"Harold, I'm not asking for permission. I am giving you the choice to decide if you want to be part of this journey with us," Thando stated firmly.

Thando recognized that their relationship thrived on a delicate balance of give and take. Seeking permission created intimacy and security for the other partner. With her decision to move forward, Thando wanted to offer Harold the choice to decide whether he would spend his life and their lives honoring her grandmother's legacy. She loved him enough to release him from the constraints of her vision. There was no room for negotiation.

"I'll begin tomorrow with Lungi, and thank you for standing by me," Thando said matter-of-factly, walking toward the nursery to attend to Zhara, who was already demanding attention with her cooing sounds. Thando knew that Harold was not thrilled about the speed at which things were progressing. She appreciated his commitment and support for her and their family.

X. HOME

Thando lay on her bed, feeling the softness of the mattress beneath her. The moonlight seeped through the curtains, casting gentle shadows on the walls. She appreciated the quiet, a break from her usual hectic routine.

She welcomed the brief morning relief from her motherly duties to Zhara, and there were no work deadlines to close or urgent emails to respond to. It felt like time had paused momentarily, allowing her to breathe.

The sudden, jarring noise of drilling disturbed the calm, abruptly pulling Thando back to reality. It reminded her that peace was fleeting and often disrupted, that the tranquility she felt came from within herself, a part she hadn't paid attention to during that period.

Thando's life has had its ups and downs. Some days, she felt hopeful and excited about the future, while others days left her questioning her choices and purpose. Her emotions are unpredictable, making her feel lost at times.

During her emotional ups and downs, Thando found unexpected comfort in a place close to her heart—the ongoing construction work happening in her childhood neighborhood. Walking through the streets she knew so well, she couldn't help but notice the incredible changes happening around her. A new school was taking shape daily, showing that people were investing in the future. Nearby, workers carefully installed solar panels, proving a commitment to eco-friendly living. The community seemed to move positively, becoming greener and more environmentally conscious.

Thando observed the project's progress and found a sense of tranquility. The sight of trees being planted, their roots firmly gripping the soil, and native plants bursting with vibrant hues filled her with a profound sense of pride and purpose. The burgeoning growth and development in her surroundings ignited a spark within her. Each new tree and solar panel reinforced her belief in her capacity to positively impact her community.

Every additional tree and solar panel strengthened her, fueling her inspiration. The ongoing construction work became a symbol of progress and change for Thando. It reminded her that personal growth thrives on the currency of change. She became deeply interested in the project and eagerly awaited each monthly update. Whether through reports or conference calls with Lungi, the project manager, she immersed herself in the progress made and challenges faced.

Seeing her childhood sanctuary transform into an educational center and a place promoting sustainable living gave Thando a renewed sense of purpose. She started to view her journey as a work in progress, with ups and downs, setbacks, and breakthroughs— just like the construction project. These fluctuations, though sometimes challenging, pushed her towards a future filled with promise. The construction site became a source of inspiration, reminding Thando that even with the changes in her own life, she had the power to make a meaningful difference—both within herself and in the world around her.

Thando, with her proactive approach, took on the responsibility of updating everyone on the project. She diligently created detailed reports and organized conference calls with Lungi. Recognizing the importance of keeping everyone informed, Thando ensured monthly updates were sent out, fostering a sense of involvement among the stakeholders.

Thando deeply valued Lungi's active involvement in the project. Lungi didn't just share information—she also contributed her valuable insights and expertise, which significantly pushed the project forward. Thando made a point to credit Lungi for her hard work and dedication, recognizing her as a pivotal part of the team.

Once he settled in, Harold's infectious enthusiasm for the project had a great impact. His passion, which even Thando hadn't anticipated, inspired everyone involved. Harold's energy and positivity were contagious, instilling a strong belief in the project's potential.

*

However, Thando hit a roadblock when she faced resistance from the local community regarding the eco-houses. Despite her efforts to gain their trust and support, residents had genuine concerns. They worried that the eco-houses would be too expensive and change their way of life. While they liked the idea of environmentally friendly homes, they felt the upscale versions were out of reach.

Deeply rooted in their community, the residents appreciated their simple and sustainable lifestyle. They found fulfillment in living harmoniously with nature, devoid of Western luxuries like solar panels, ornate gardens, and sprawling shopping centers. Their contentment stemmed from a collective belief that happiness could be found in the simplicity of life's essentials.

As Thando strolled down the streets she'd known since childhood, a wave of tension rippled through her. She'd braced herself for some resistance to the eco-houses project, but the depth of opposition caught her off guard.

Thando sat among her neighbors in community meetings, their faces etched with concern. Their words came in hesitant bursts, magnified by a passion for their way of life. They spoke of a deep connection to the land, where simplicity and sustainability were cherished. The idea of shiny solar panels and modern designs felt foreign, even threatening, to their traditional values.

She watched as they gesticulated, their hands painting a vivid picture of their worries. They fretted about rising costs, about being priced out of their neighborhood. The thought of sleek, high-tech homes replacing their cozy abodes left them feeling uprooted and anxious.

Thando's earnest attempts to ease their fears and bridge the gap between their values and the project's objectives, but she couldn't shake the weight of uncertainty. While eco-friendly living struck a chord with the community, the practical implications felt daunting, like a distant reality they weren't sure they were ready to embrace.

The clash of values presented Thando with a tricky situation. She needed to find a way to respect the residents' traditions while also showing them the advantages of eco-friendly ideas.

Skepticism surrounding the project grew into a tempest, a storm of emotions that led protesters to flock to the development site passionately expressing their concerns, clutching signs and posters with slogans "Protect our Heritage" and "Protect our Land." The protests attracted negative media attention, casting a shadow on Thando and her project. The media coverage often portrayed the community's concerns and the protests in a critical light, further complicating Thando's efforts to gain support and address the community's grievances.

Harold forged a special bond with the community, taking the time to understand their concerns and empathize with their resistance to change. He prioritized listening to their worries and effectively conveyed their sentiments to Thando. Their shared conviction ran deep, compelling Thando to make a tough call—to pause the project until she could address the community's concerns.

Thando's journey, marked by battles against racial and economic oppression, had made her resilient. Yet, facing opposition from her beloved community caught her off guard, shaking her certainty. The unexpected resistance left her uncertain, unsure of her next move.

Encountering resistance from her people struck a chord with Thando. She had anticipated challenges from external sources but not from her community. This forced her to confront a dilemma, questioning her assumptions and leaving her at a crossroads. Her past experiences added complexity, intensifying her uncertainty about the best path forward.

As Thando wrestled with the situation, she realized the importance of careful consideration and finding common ground. Building trust and support required a delicate balance, where the voices of the community needed to be heard and respected.

*

"I understand your frustration. If we do not take action, one of those profit-driven global corporations will likely exploit our community without considering the people," She Said, Expressing her concerns about the backlash she faced from her community.

Equally frustrated, Harold disagreed with Thando's emotional perspective on their situation, saying, "But right now, they perceive you as part of the problem, Thando. They see you through the same lens as those corporations." Understanding the emotional toll it would take, he realized that moving back to New York after aligning his goals with Thando's vision would be challenging.

Thando acknowledged Harold's viewpoint, saying, "I hear what you're saying, Harold." But Harold insisted, "No, Thando, you need to truly listen. We must find a solution that benefits both the community and your vision."

Thando's emotional guard finally crumbled as she admitted, "I hear you." She had been suppressing her fears and doubts in the face of adversity. For the first time since they moved to Duduza, she acknowledged her uncertainty about the future. She questioned whether she could bear the criticism from her people, who cherished her grandmother's legacy and accused her of tarnishing it.

"I understand your thoughts on failure, Thando. But it's not too late. We can still find a resolution that benefits everyone," Harold encouraged her. He informed her about an upcoming community meeting at the town hall, led by the community spokesperson, urging her to attend and genuinely listen to the concerns raised.

With a soft utterance, Thando promised, "I will." Disappointed in herself, she wondered aloud, '*How did I become someone perceived to be selling out her community?*' She felt she had let down both her people and her grandmother's legacy.

"Thando, you're not like them. The narrative has been misconstrued. You still have the opportunity to change it," Harold reassured her, emphasizing the importance of embracing failure as a gift.

*

"You must see what you came to do through to the end," Thando's aunt advised, gently adjusting the traditional blanket draped over her shoulders. Her husband, sitting beside her, nodded in agreement. Harold had approached Thando's uncle, a respected elder in the family, to help convey the community's concerns to Thando.

"Mshana, kunendhlela yokwenza izinto, ukujabulisi ukubona umphakathi nomdeni wani uxabane," Thando's uncle emphasized his concerns in their native language after gathering insights from other community elders and becoming aware of the resistance within the community.

Thando buried her face in her hands and said, "I'm not sure where I missed the mark, Malume. I'm contemplating calling off the entire project and returning to the U.S." Tears welled up in her eyes as she handed Zhara, her young daughter, to Harold, who excused himself from the family discussion to give them privacy.

"Nxese Mshana," her uncle offered comforting words. "The elders have informed me that you have reached an agreement. There's no need to make an emotional decision."

Uncertain, Thando expressed her doubts, saying, "I don't know, Malume. I feel like they agreed because of your involvement, not because they genuinely believe in the project."

Her aunt stepped in to clarify, "They do believe in the project, and they understand your motivations. They wanted to ensure the community's values and well-being were protected. We're all here to support you, and you know that."

Interrupting the conversation, Uncle Musa reminded Thando of the importance of preserving their traditions and culture, saying, "Inkinga Mshana is that when you kids go study outside the village, you often return having lost touch with our traditions. How we do things is just as important as what we do. It goes beyond legal paperwork; it requires community support."

Thando took a moment to absorb their words and then said, "I hear you, Malume and Auntie, and I appreciate your support and your visit." She embraced them tightly, grateful for their presence and encouragement.

They walked out of the house, and her aunt admired the transformation of her mother-in-law's house into a beautiful sanctuary, noting, "Thando, you've made the place look like a haven." They shared a heartfelt embrace, with her uncle expressing how proud he was of her work and the vision she had for the community.

*

With the first rays of sunlight streaming through her window, Thando woke up, a surge of courage pulsing through her veins. The words "Think Globally, infuse excellence locally" echoed within her, a phrase she chanted like a mantra that she had discovered within the pages of countless business articles she read to stay ahead of the global economy. While the name of the author eluded her memory, the profound impact of those words remained etched in her heart.

Thando set her sights on a meeting with Amit Patel, a prominent community leader infamous for opposing the very development project. There were whispers that he feared the proposed changes would divert attention from his taverns, which served as his primary sources of income. These rumors suggested that he controlled the local shebeens, coercing them into selling his alcohol and extorting money through "protection fees" imposed by the thugs on his payroll. Her uncle had also disclosed another shocking piece of information—Amit's involvement in instigating protests. It was alleged that he paid hooligans in the neighborhood to cause trouble, further complicating the situation and jeopardizing any chance of a peaceful dialogue.

Thando grappled with her determination to find a solution that kept her going, even though Harold disagreed. She wanted to bridge the gap with Amit. And show him the long-term benefits the development projects could bring to the entire community. Thando believed that by promoting open communication and understanding, they could reach a mutually beneficial outcome.

Despite Harold's strong disagreement, Thando's resolve to resolve the situation and restart the project pushed her to disregard his advice and decide to go meet Amit. She kept her plan hidden, not telling anyone about her intentions, acting as if she were simply going on a regular trip to the supermarket. Thando got into her car and made her way to the city where Amit had his office.

*

Her GPS announced her arrival at the destination, and a flush of nervous anticipation came over her, causing her heart to flutter. Uncertain about what awaited her inside, she paused for a moment to collect herself, taking a deep breath to steady her nerves.

She stepped out of the car, and instantly, the bustling noise of the busy road met Thando. Street vendors claimed every available spot around the building, adding to the vibrant chaos of the atmosphere. The chaotic energy of the surroundings seemed to mirror the worn-out appearance of the office building itself. Her attention was immediately drawn to the unmistakable signs of wear and tear. Cracked windows scarred the once-smooth façade of the high-rise, with graffiti marking the entrance. The sight of the door being violently pushed open, with a noticeable footprint left behind, served as a chilling reminder of what had happened.

Clutching her purse tightly, Thando made her way into the building, taking careful, calculated steps that mirrored her mindset. She entered the lobby and reached out to press the elevator button that would take her to the 13th floor. Standing beside her was a tall, muscular black man, his physique resembling that of a seasoned bodybuilder. His dark skin gleamed under the dim lights, accentuating the defined muscles in his arms and shoulders, which bulged beneath his tightly fitting uniform. A holstered gun rested securely at his hip, and his hand occasionally touched its handle, his posture alert and watchful.

The security guy insisted on escorting her to Amit's penthouse-like office. His presence heightened her anxiety, which sharply contrasted with the opulence of the destination she was about to reach.

The doors of the elevator opened on the 13th floor, and Thando and the security guard walked into Amit's office, finding him already seated, his impatience evident in his posture. In contrast to the guard, Amit looked different, and Thando understood why he needed the security presence. His hair, thinning and peppered with gray, was combed back meticulously, his face carved by the wrinkles that hinted at years of experience. His dark brown eyes gleamed with a calculating intensity, framed by bushy eyebrows. He was dressed in a custom suit that shaped his stocky frame, the dark fabric contrasting sharply with the multiple glittering gold chains around his neck. An oversized gold watch on his left wrist, its face shimmering under the office lights.

Amit's posture was rigid as he sat behind his mahogany desk, a glass of whiskey in hand, his fingers wrapped tightly around it. The pungent aroma of the liquor was strong in the room, mingling with the scent of leather from the plush chairs and the polished wood of the desk. He offered Thando a drink with a nod, his lips curving into a thin, patronizing smile. His eyes, however, remained narrow, watching her every move. The extravagance of his office, with its luxurious furnishings and elaborate decor, echoed his demeanor, exuding an aura of self-importance that clung to him like a second skin.

Amit's ostentatious display of wealth was hard to miss. Thando observed how his outward appearance seemed to mirror his demeanor, exuding an air of grandiosity that permeated the room.

She politely declined the glass of whiskey, choosing instead to take a seat, her focus unwavering. The room was adorned with lavish decorations, reflecting Amit Patel's ostentatious taste. Thando leaned forward, acknowledging Amit's presence and expressing her gratitude for his willingness to meet.

"Mr. Patel, I appreciate you taking the time to meet with me. I believe we must address the concerns surrounding the development change".

Lounging back, wearing a smug expression, Amit let out an authoritative cough. "My dearest Thando, I want to understand why you think your fancy projects will bring any benefit to our community."

"Mr. Patel Sir," Thando said, trying to maintain respectful decorum in the conversation, "This project isn't just about fancy changes. It's about sustainable growth and creating opportunities for our community to thrive. I've seen firsthand how similar initiatives have uplifted other regions." Remaining calm, Thando clarified that her projects were not mere superficial changes.

Raising his black bushy eyebrows, he says, "And who will truly benefit, Thando? Will it be our hardworking villagers who have relied on traditional ways of life for generations? Or will it only be those with money and power who reap the rewards?"

Thando said, "That's why I've taken great care to ensure the project brings inclusive growth. It will create jobs for my people, improve infrastructure, and provide educational opportunities for our youth. We can preserve our heritage while embracing progress. I understand your business interests, but with all due respect, these are my people, and I believe I know what is best for us. "Thando's frustration grew with each passing moment as she observed Amit's arrogance and his position as an outsider benefitting from the community without truly understanding their needs. She saw through his ulterior motives, sensing the greed that powered his actions. Amit, being of Indian descent, had never lived within the community, making him out of touch with their struggles and hopes.

Thando sensed his self-serving motives, aiming to take advantage of the community for his gain. "What are you implying?" Amit's voice thundered through the room, his anger palpable. His face flushed with fury as he glared at Thando, the intensity of his emotions boiling over. The air in the office grew heavy with tension, thick with Amit's indignation.

Taken aback by Amit's explosive reaction, Thando felt anger rising within her. She had hit a nerve, exposing his true intentions. Her heart raced, and her palms grew clammy, forcing herself to stay composed.

Summoning every ounce of courage, her voice quivered with determination. "I'm not implying anything," she shot back, her eyes meeting Amit's fiery gaze. "I can see through your selfish motives, Amit. You're exploiting our community for your gain, and I won't stay silent."

Amit's anger intensified, and his face contorted with rage. He rose from his seat, pointing a finger at Thando, his voice venomous. "Get out!" he bellowed; his words laced with contempt. The force of his command sent shockwaves through Thando, her breath catching in her throat.

Thando, her anger still smoldering within her, met Amit's gaze one last time, her eyes shimmering with defiance. Without uttering a word, she turned on her heels and walked away, leaving behind the remnants of their intense confrontation.

She hurriedly made her way to her car with her heart pounding in her chest, fear gripping her every step. She resisted the urge to glance back, afraid of what she might see lurking in the shadows behind her. The sound of the security guard closing the door behind her echoed in her ears, a sharp bang that heightened her unease. Reaching her car, Thando fumbled with the keys, her hands trembling with nervousness. Without taking a moment to buckle her seatbelt, she started the engine and accelerated away from the scene. She gripped the steering wheel harder, trying to shake off the worries and fears buzzing in her head.

As soon as she got onto the Highway, a mist of calm washed over her. The rhythmic hum of the engine and the steady flow of traffic around her provided a temporary pause from the intense emotions that had consumed her moments ago. Her mind continued to race with questions and uncertainties despite the temporary calmness. What had she stumbled upon? What secrets lay hidden behind the façade she had dared to challenge? The unknown loomed large in her thoughts, casting a shadow over her newfound sense of calm. Her stomach churned, and each breath felt shallow as if the unknown threatened to suffocate her.

With a steady hand, she reached for her phone and dialed Harold's number.

After a few rings, Harold answered the call, his voice filled with warmth and concern. "Thando, is everything alright?" he asked, concerned when she had been unreachable for the past four hours. The sound of Harold's voice was a much-needed balm to soothe her frayed nerves.

Thando took a moment to collect herself, drawing strength from Harold's presence, even if it was through the phone. "I am ok, I went to meet Amit," she replied, her voice steady, tinged with a hint of vulnerability,

Harold's concern deepened, and he listened attentively as Thando relayed the details of the intense encounter and her subsequent decision to continue her journey.

"And Zhara," Thando continued, her voice laced with genuine concern, "How is she holding up? I can't shake off the worry for her safety with all of this."

"Zhara is okay, but what time will you be home? We need to decide whether to inform the police or put out a restraining order."

Thando paused for a moment, her mind processing the weight of Harold's words. Concern for her safety and the potential need for legal protection weighed heavily on her thoughts. She understood the gravity of the situation and the importance of taking necessary precautions.

"Harold, I appreciate your concern," Thando replied, her voice laced with gratitude and worry. "Let's not take any chances. We should consider involving the authorities and exploring the possibility of obtaining a restraining order. I'll be home as soon as I can, but I can't give you an exact time at the moment. Please keep an eye on Zhara and take all necessary measures to ensure her safety."

*

Thando's heart raced in her chest, pounding with fear. The sudden impact at the back of her car startled her, jolting panic through her body. Her hands shook as she tightly gripped the steering wheel, trying to regain control of her racing thoughts. Her phone slipped from her hand and fell to the floor, a casualty of her mounting distress. She quickly glanced in the rearview mirror and froze as her eyes met the gaze of the driver behind her. Their frantic gestures and urgent waves filled her with the perception of danger, intensifying her suspicion and unease. Her recent encounter with Amit is still fresh in her mind, heightening her belief that she was being chased, trapped in a world of unknown and threatening intentions.

A rush of adrenaline flowed through her bloodstream., compelling her to press her foot down hard on the accelerator. The engine responded with a roar as the speedometer rapidly climbed, blurring the passing scenery into a chaotic blur.

Up ahead, another car stubbornly blocked Thando's path, refusing to yield.

Fear twisted her insides into knots when she realized they were working together—a chilling revelation that intensified the surrounding danger.

Her mind raced, torn between the options of stopping or continuing to drive forward.

The nearest village was miles away, and the deserted road amplified her isolation. Panic surged within her as she desperately searched for a way out of the treacherous predicament. The sun beat down brightly, making it increasingly challenging for approaching vehicles to notice her distress signals with the vehicle obstructing her way.

Thando was indecisive. The instinct to seek help and find safety battled with the grim reality that she was trapped in a potentially perilous situation. She carefully considered her choices, acutely aware that time was slipping away.

In a desperate bid for assistance, Thando repeatedly flashed her lights, hoping to catch the attention of passing drivers. Still, the glaring daylight hindered her efforts, obscuring her distress signals beyond the car and blocking her path.

Thando held onto the steering wheel tightly, her knuckles turning white as she desperately tried to control the car. But the other vehicles ahead, working together, were too much for her to handle. They were speeding recklessly, overpowering her and leaving her helpless against their actions.

The speedometer kept climbing, matching the escalating danger that pounded in Thando's chest. Despite her efforts, she couldn't regain control. The car swerved violently, veering off the road, and panic surged within her. Everything was happening in a chaotic blur as her car rolled over, each rotation intensifying her fear and disorientation.

The sound of metal screeching and glass shattering filled the air, mingling with Thando's cries of disbelief. The familiar interior of her car transformed into a hurricane of chaos, turning into an unrecognizable and terrifying scene.

In that horrifying moment, Thando's body jolted with the impact of the rollover. The crash left her dazed and bruised, her senses overwhelmed by the cacophony of noise and the sudden halt of movement. The world around her seemed to stand still, leaving her disoriented and struggling to comprehend the magnitude of the situation.

*

"We rushed her to the ICU, she was slipping into a coma" The somber words cut through the air, tearing at the fragile remains of hope that Harold and her uncle clung to. The devastating news sent shockwaves through their beings, threatening to consume them in an abyss of anguish.

In that instant, their lives shattered into countless fragments, their hearts splintered into irreparable pieces. The ground beneath them seemed to crumble, leaving them suspended in a void of disbelief and despair. The world grew dim, robbed of its vibrancy by the sudden uncertainty surrounding someone so cherished.

Harold and her uncle were caught off guard, standing frozen in shock and disbelief, unable to understand the sudden and tragic turn of events. Just days ago, they had been filled with hope and encouragement, supporting Thando's progress and celebrating her accomplishments.

Time seemed to stand still as they grappled with the incomprehensible loss, their minds consumed by memories of Thando's infectious laughter, her charisma, and her radiant spirit.

The air hung heavy with weariness and despair, and Harold, finally catching his breath after an eternity, uttered a single word that carried the weight of a thousand emotions and a thousand implicit words—"Zhara!"

Harold sat by Thando's side. He felt overwhelmed by caring for his daughter. He was also worried about his wife's condition. Hope had once filled the hospital room. Now, uncertainty hung heavy, casting a shadow over their once-bright future.

But with family and friends by his side, Harold found strength in their love and support. Every day, he held Thando's hand. His whispered words blended with the prayers of those around him. They all hoped for her recovery.

Through all the ups and downs, their daughter Zhara became a source of light. Her visits brought a sense of warmth and optimism to the sterile hospital room. Her belief in her mom's recovery shone through in her drawings and gestures.

Time passed, and Thando remained in her coma; uncertainty loomed large. Despite their hope and the support of loved ones, the future remained unclear.

*

As time stretched on and Thando lingered in her coma, the hospital room became a refuge—a place where hope flickered like a candle in the darkness of uncertainty. Despite the challenges and moments when despair threatened to overwhelm them, Harold and their loved ones clung to each other, finding strength in the memories of Thando's infectious laughter and comforting hugs.

Through it all, Zhara remained a ray of sunshine. With every visit, she breathed life into the room, infusing it with energy and vitality. Her giggles and gentle, soft hands were oblivious to the possibility of death. Her vibrant drawings served as tangible reminders of the love and optimism that filled their hearts.

Then, one miraculous day, Thando stirred. Her eyes fluttered open to the sight of her family gathered around her, their faces alight with joy and relief. At that moment, as she basked in their embrace and heard their cheers, Thando understood the depth of her journey. It wasn't just a tale of struggle but a testament to the resilience and determination that had carried her through the darkest times.

As she began her journey toward recovery, Thando knew that her story would resonate with other black women navigating their paths. She believed that dreams could be realized with perseverance and support.

Thando stepped back into the world. Each step forward was a stroke of defiance against adversity, a declaration of her unwavering faith in the boundless potential of black women to overcome any obstacle and achieve greatness. She painted her dreams with bold strokes of passion and conviction; she knew that her story was not just one of struggle but of love, hope, and the undeniable power of the human spirit.

Thando's Corporate Blueprint: Evaluate, Thrive, Exit

Ready to start over, Thando decided to create her own set of rules to navigate life's twists and turns. She called it her corporate blueprint for success.

She felt empowered to face whatever challenges life threw her way. She was ready to write a new story.

1. **Make Self-Care** a Priority: Your well-being is not just important; it's a priority. Don't view stress and overwork as a sign of dedication. There's no glory in feeling mentally and physically drained. Strive for a healthy balance and seek support outside of work when needed. Remember, your health and happiness are crucial to your success.

2. **Have an Exit Strategy**: Start with an exit plan in mind. Every six months, review that plan and make changes if necessary. Having an exit strategy doesn't mean you plan to quit right away. It means you're prepared, in control, and ready to make the best decisions for your career.

3. **Don't ignore Corporate Politics**: Gain a deep understanding of the power dynamics within your organization. Strategically build relationships, navigate office politics, and position yourself for career growth. By understanding the game, you can play it to your advantage and make informed decisions about your career path.

4. **Be Proud of Your Uniqueness:** Don't let anyone make you feel like you have to fit into a mold. Your unique experiences, perspectives, and cultural background are your superpowers, and they can make you stand out in the workplace.

5. **Blow your own horn**: In meetings, negotiations, and performance evaluations, don't be afraid to voice your opinions and assert your worth. Be bold and keep score of all the fantastic things you have done to move the business forward. Advocate for fair treatment, equal opportunities, and recognition of your contributions. For instance, if you're being overlooked for a promotion, speak up and present your case.

6. **Negotiate with Confidence:** Research your market and use data, when possible, to negotiate your salary, promotions, or job offers. Research industry standards and be prepared to articulate the value you bring to the table. Do it with confidence and assertiveness.

7. **Use the Employee Resource Groups:** Use the resources available at work for support but be objective in these forums. Speak your truth, but don't be emotional. If unsure, consult a professional counselor outside the organization to help unpack your perspective.

8. **Don't ignore Microaggressions and Bias. Don't** gaslight yourself—avoid dismissing your own experiences. Learn to identify the right moments to stand up for yourself and seek equitable treatment. Develop effective strategies to confront microaggressions, unconscious bias, and discriminatory practices in the workplace.

9. **Get a Mentor:** Look for a mentor outside of work or ask someone senior to be your sponsor or outside the company to get an objective view. A mentor who understands your experiences can offer valuable insights and support.

10. **Lawyer Up:** When all else fails or if you lack confidence in navigating certain situations, seek legal advice from a trusted attorney. They can clarify your rights, options, and potential courses of action, ensuring you're protected and empowered in your professional decisions.

Hey Black Child

Useni Eugene Perkins

Hey Black Child,
Do you know who you are?
Who you really are?
Do you know you can be
What you want to be?
If you try to be
what you can be.

Hey Black Child,
Do you know where you're going?
Where you're really going?
Do you know you can learn
What you want to learn?
If you try to learn
What you can learn?

Hey Black Child,
Do you know you are strong?
I mean really strong?
Do you know you can do
What you want to do?
If you try to do
What you can do?

Hey Black Child,
Be what you can be
Learn what you must learn

Do what you can do
And tomorrow your nation will be
what you want it to be

{ 196 }